Special thanks to Julia Ringo.

Published by Semiotext(e)
PO BOX 629, South Pasadena, CA 91031
www.semiotexte.com

Cover Art: Issy Wood, *Car interior / For once*, 2019, Oil on linen, 220 × 160 × 4 cm. Image © Issy Wood 2025, courtesy the artist; Carlos/Ishikawa, London; and Michael Werner Gallery, New York.

Cover Design: Lauren Mackler and Ivan Gaytan
Layout: Hedi El Kholti
ISBN: 978-1-63590-257-0

10 9 8 7 6 5 4 3 2 1

Distributed by the MIT Press, Cambridge, MA., and London, England.
Printed in the United States of America

Grand Rapids

Natasha Stagg

semiotext(e)

On *Grosse Income*, Bella is telling everyone to leave her house. She can't stand the hypocrisy, she says. She'd just wanted someone to be real. It looks like she's describing something that no one has ever heard of. The faces of each woman in the cast, plus a gay male friend, a husband, and a daughter, take up the screen, one by one, in reaction to what Bella is saying. "This party is lame anyway," says Rachel. No music plays, and it sounds like someone is washing dishes. Other people are talking to one another as if nothing is going on. They are party guests, but none of them are introduced. Barely recognizable, in the background, is the politician.

It was the first time a person I personally knew was on television. I watched as he had a conversation with a man that looked about his age, meaning old. I wondered where his wife was. I'd know her from the one photo I'd seen of him, the one on his website that said he was running for local office. On-screen, the politician talked, leaning closer to this old man, who was eating snacks with one hand off a small plate that he held with the other. They both disappeared behind the main action.

"Hey." Norma's voice was right behind me. "Can I talk to you for a second?"

I muted the TV. She sat down next to me on the floor.

"We want you to know that you can stay here for as long as you want. I know John makes it sound like he makes all the rules, but you and I know that's not true. I'm going to do whatever feels right, and what feels right is that you have a place here. And when you're on breaks in college—"

"I don't want to think about college right now," I said.

"I know. It's early yet."

We sat in silence for a time. I turned the sound on because the show was back.

"One more thing."

I looked up at Norma.

"Can you mute that again?"

I considered saying no. Bella was telling her side of the story in a confessional. I'd missed so much of the episode already.

"Your mother wanted me to give you her diary." Norma paused again for dramatic effect. "But not until you're eighteen. She said eighteen because you'll be an adult, and there are some things in it that are kind of, well, adult."

"You've read it?"

"We told each other everything. Sisters do."

I looked back at the quiet TV.

"I'm not telling you this to hold it over you, I'm telling you because it's what she wanted. Can you look at me? For you to stay here. With us. At least until you're eighteen."

"Where else would I go?"

The phone was for me. It was a coworker, one I had never met, asking if I could cover for her. She felt sick and had to leave. I could be there in twenty-five minutes or so, I said. The nursing home was only a fifteen-minute walk away, out the stained-glass front door and down the long gravel driveway, along a road edged with fenced-in fields and through a neighborhood of dead ends—cul-de-sacs, I learned. Where I worked, one of the Berrylawn buildings, looked like just another bulky house in the neighborhood, except it had less windows. The parking lot was hidden in the back.

After clocking in, getting scolded for not wearing a hat or bandana, and going back to the office to take a hairnet from a carboard box on the desk there, I went to the dining room to collect all the stiff burgundy napkins and threadbare white washcloths used at breakfast. The napkins were all on the tables, and most of them were still in the shapes they had been in when they were set there: triangular wings. The washcloths were strewn around the floor, soggy with food and drool.

I picked up the napkins first and used them as claws to pick up the cloths, throwing everything in a canvas bin that rolled around the room. In Assisted Living, the Berrylawn building for slightly younger residents, where I'd started, the burgundy napkins were smoothed out by more nimble fingers and draped over laps. The unfolded wings swooped around corners of mouths and settled down into buttoned shirt collars. There, the white washcloth bibs, like surrender flags, were only in case of emergencies. Here, in the Berrylawn Care Center, there were fewer formalities.

One of the resident nurses that had shuffled in and out of Berrylawn so quickly that I forgot her face and name had said that "these people ain't completely nuts; mostly they just can't accept where they at. I don't know about you, but I'd have some trouble with it." That was the first time I'd really considered the residents' histories—their lives, their pasts, their children, their grandchildren, and the drug-induced lies that stood for those things that were once real to them.

Ricky Platz, I was told, was the only resident regularly visited by a husband. This statistic was different at the other Berrylawn, too. Arnold Platz lived in Assisted Living, just across the grass. He was tall and pale, with reddish cheeks and gray eyes, and when he walked, he had to brace himself. He looked like he was always on the sliding metal plates in a carnival funhouse and his bright white hair curled up and away from his head, reminding me of a Van Gogh tree. He stood at the windowed doors of the dining hall and furrowed his brow, his expression going from anxious to perplexed, while I cleaned.

Eventually, an RN would lead Ricky out in her wheelchair and then turn her around to push her back to her room, Arnold following behind. Ricky had a dry sense of humor and she drooled relentlessly. Once, she physically pulled me aside and asked me to try to find "the food in this food." Later, maybe on the same day, she took hold of my sleeve and said, "You don't belong here, girl. Can you take me upstairs?"

"This building has one floor," I answered. Ricky looked at me like I had told her to go to hell. Most RNs disliked Ricky because of her grasping hands that knocked over everything in their path. If I had had to wheel around the residents like the RNs did, maybe I would pick different favorites, too.

After binning the napkins, I tried to calm down one of Cal van Duren's temper tantrums, which was going on a little too long. It was not part of my job to tend to the residents in this way, but this flare-up was occurring simultaneously with a screaming fit across the room that was also being ignored, and Cal seemed easier to handle than Dennis Shandler, one of the only male residents. Cal's lips were crusty and thin, her glasses comically askew. "Help me, help me, help me," she yelped. Her bib hung loosely around her neck, having dodged any food that had been dropped or spit during her feeding. When Cal saw me kneel beside her, she didn't quite acknowledge me, but she did quiet down a little.

"How can I help you?" I asked.

"Help me, help—I got the wrong chair. This isn't mine."

"It's the only one with a neck brace attached to it. It's yours." Saying "neck brace" aloud to Cal felt wrong, but there it was, a neck brace.

"Maybe. Can you take me upstairs?"

"I can't," I said. I didn't try to explain to her, too, that there was only one floor here. Maybe Ricky had started a rumor.

"Just take me outside, then."

"She wants to go outside, and I don't blame her," said Anne Morris, another resident in a wheelchair, who had snuck up behind us. "If you take her, take me, too, and just roll me into oncoming traffic."

I appreciated the word *oncoming* in the sentence, the cadence it created.

I'd never really met the politician, but I felt that I knew him better than I knew a lot of people. My old friend Gina and I found him in a chat room. This was back in Ypsilanti, when I first lived there. We would talk with him when we were together, using my screen name, and eventually, I'd message him whenever I was by myself at the computer. Sometimes I couldn't respond to something for days, and then he would tell me it devastated him. I loved reading that. Then, sometimes, he wouldn't respond, and I hated that, but I never told him so.

It was us who had started to message him privately. Amid a lot of emoticons and dicks made from Bs and equal signs and Ds in the chat room, he was asking if anyone had read any good books lately. He said he had just finished "A heartbreaking work of staggering genius." Gina and I liked that phrase. "What was the genius book you just read?" we asked him, as an opener. He repeated the phrase, and we asked, "But what was it called?" Together, we constructed our messages aloud and then I typed them. He told us he was hoping to find some friends, some recommendations, and some fun.

"What did you do on the 4th of July?" we asked.

"I spent the day with family, for better and worse. What did you do?" He was a fast typist, sending long messages, with punctuation and without abbreviations.

"Nothing."

"Sounds pretty rough. I'm all for making the most of holidays. It's my only real time off."

"I have summer off," we wrote.

"Hey, it's summer now, isn't it? What are you up to tonight, since you have it off?"

"I am with a friend now."

"So, you're there together, looking at the same screen? Hi, friend."

"Hi."

He continued to send us message after message as we giggled and argued over what our answers should be. We learned that he was running for local political office and that he lived in Grosse Pointe. He sent us a link to a website with his photo on it. He looked very old, we said to each other. He was married, we noticed.

"What do you want to see happen in the next four years?" he joked.

"To see this girl in our class dead," we joked back.

"I could arrange that," he said, followed by a winking emoticon.

It was exhilarating, the speed with which he responded to us, even if we left him alone for a while to look at something else on the internet. Whenever we came back to the chat window, he had sent several messages. He asked what we were doing, how we looked, how well we knew one another, what types of foods we liked, and if we were going to spend the night together.

"We are having a sleepover," I typed.

"You're making me jealous," he wrote. "It's not fair."

We were covering each other's mouths to stop our laughter from waking my mother. That was before I moved cities, moved schools, fell out of touch with Gina, back when my mother was still alive.

I suppose I'm telling you all this because you asked. That question, *Where are you from?* The coded proposition: prove it, something, depending. A person is from the place they were born, where they learned to read, lost their virginity, *came of age*. And when I told you where I'm from, you made a face I've seen before, and it revolted me. I can see you tidying up my background, my youth, in a phrase, and no matter what it may be—*working class, suburban, white trash, middle America*—it doesn't work. No, I am not a special star, for which one of those phrases isn't applicable—I can see you coming up with more: *army brat, academia, second generation*—it's that these words always call to mind others, and the conversation circles a putrid drain.

Do I like living in Chicago, now? Not exactly. It was my dream until it came true. And it is still a dream, every time I take Lakeshore Drive and traffic clears away, letting through a frosty sun that sparkles on the water that goes out as far as an ocean because it has no end. What these structures, these beautiful houses and their grinning hedges, mean to me is more than you can imagine. And maybe they are something else to you, something oppressive or elusive or boring. Would I ever move to another city? What kind of question is that? All I know is that whenever I move to a new apartment, I detest the one I left, the one I used to love because it was mine.

We still talked about it all the time, but if I was being honest, not a lot had changed after September 11th. Everyone was so worried that there would be a war here, and yet, after days of the news channel being left on, life went back to normal, except that I had to switch schools because my mother was dying.

The rest of my sophomore year went by quickly. Most of what happened during it was like a playback of distant memories, but in the present. I guess I was out of school for weeks doing things like picking out a coffin with Norma, going to a funeral that was in a blank Protestant church crammed with bouquets, then the visitation in another room full of even more flowers, with no time to wonder where any of this stuff came from and who set it all up. Before she was even dead, I was meeting with a lawyer about the will, seeing paperwork about money matters, which ended up not mattering at all, since she didn't have any savings left after moving. Then, I was taking all my things and her things to the house I'd known all my life as my rich aunt and uncle's. My new bedroom was in a finished basement that stored Christmas decorations and snowboarding gear.

When my parents divorced, my mother, Sheila, got full custody of me, so we moved to Grand Rapids to be closer to her sister, Norma. I hated Sheila for moving me, but then she got cancer, so I had to forgive her for everything. She was angrier than I was, anyway, because she was finally free from her husband, and I was growing up, so she had all this time to herself, time she'd really wanted, but then she was dying.

I never even questioned if I would be sent back to my father, because he had moved away, too, and we didn't call each other on the phone except for on holidays. I don't think I even knew his email address, if he had one, then. It was sort of Sheila's dying wish that I would stay away from him and become close to Norma, who Sheila said was like a younger her. That turned out to be not true at all. I hated Norma, her husband, and their children. I hated how loud they were and how Christian they were, and I hated how vocal each one of them was about missing Sheila, even though it was like they barely knew her, the way they'd describe her.

I don't even know what happened to Sheila's and my old furniture. It nauseated me, thinking about how much work it took to get the Formica kitchen table, the chairs with woven seats, the dusty yellow couch, the standup mirror, my bed, her bed, and my dresser all the way across the state. Everything we owned was such garbage. We should have just thrown it away to begin with.

In my little basement room, I woke up every day hating Grand Rapids more, until it began to feel like an absurdist prison, each person in it a demented criminal I had to do my best to avoid. Sometimes I was paralyzed by sorrow for myself, my feet and mouth refusing to move. The air was gelatinous.

Every day, I got dressed in my work uniform or for school and walked to work or to the end of the driveway, where the bus would pick up my cousins and me. We sat in separate seats because there were enough empty ones for everyone. They got dropped off at middle school and I stayed on, riding through forests and hills to a building that looked like a pile of rocks held together with metal ribbons. I got off with everyone else, whoever they were, and walked down swarming halls. Each time, I thought about leaving, walking across the football field, out onto the highway, to hitchhike, or something, but I never did that. I swam the halls with the other kids; I entered rooms; I said, "Present."

My only real friend, Candy, loathed Grand Rapids as much as I did. She had moved there from Lansing when she was six. She visited her grandparents in "the capital" on holidays. Lansing was bigger, she said, and her family had lived in a house there. Now, she lived with her father and sister in one apartment and sometimes stayed with her mother in another. Once, after Candy and I got high on Robitussin and came home still tripping a little, I wrote in my diary that I was finally happy, which was sad. It was as if all the miserable things that were happening to me were so bad, they were forming a protective barrier around me, I wrote. "Does that make me less sad, being happy about being sad? I'm thrilled to be so incredibly, inconsolably sad, and I don't want to end up getting happy because of that. Does that even make sense? I don't know."

I was waiting for someone else to feel the way I did and at the same time hoping it would never happen. Nothing had hurt as bad as knowing that Sheila was dead, and every time I remembered it, it was just as bad as knowing it for the first time. It was over, everything, and then it was not, because I would be reminded of this all the time, the feeling of it being over replacing the anticipation of it ending, on a loop, like a joke. Her life is gone; your life is changed. Repeated, until you are asleep, and then you dream every night that she's alive but somehow not quite; reanimated, and not glad to be back but not upset, either; just there.

I'd thought that moving away from my friends, into a big house surrounded by horses and churches, to a new school full of spoiled blonde ingrates, gave me license to change my look to something more severe. Sheila didn't mind that I'd started lining my eyes and cutting thrift store skirts short. She appreciated the creativity. And then I lived through the ultimate severity, and so I'd earned an even harsher look. But instead of letting everyone know, I couldn't tell anyone or change anything. I practiced ways of shoving the information in some jock's face, "She's dead, asshole," but when parents came up in casual conversation, I'd look down instead, all but apologizing for even thinking about making anyone else feel as uncomfortable as I was.

I wondered if I looked like the type of girl who had a dead mother. Another girl in school had a dead father, and she brought it up as if it was her religion. She lived because her father no longer could, the brave man. He had died from cancer, too, like most parents. And when a teacher said her mother-in-law died, the whole class said something about some distant person who had been sick, or the time they'd been to the hospital to see a baby just born, and at that point I would rather lie than say my mother was dead, it felt so cheap.

We were in Candy and her sister's room, alone, high. Her hair was so red it was almost pink, cut short and swept to one side. Her eyes were yellow green, framed by lashes that were transparent but long, only visible when they moved. Candy never held still. Her hands, especially, were always fluttering. She wanted to show me something, she said. She booted up the computer and opened Napster, where she had downloaded a song by a boy who was "only fifteen, like us." She hit play. "He is so sad. The saddest. I've never heard anyone this sad, and he's fifteen." She played the song, which was of a low quality that made it sound authentic. "How could anybody be that sad?" Candy laughed.

I told her to be quiet. I felt something like a crush, but also jealousy. He was our age and could write words that defined his emotions so well. We should be doing that, I thought. We are sad, too. "Why is he so sad?" I asked.

"That's the best part," Candy said. "His songs are about his parents getting a divorce. Like, get over it."

"I was sad about that," I said, surprising myself by defending him.

"So was I," said Candy. "But, I mean, he has so much more to get sad about."

"I doubt I'll ever be more sad than I am now," I said.

"You're not happy?" It was a strange thing to ask. We were lying on her bed, looking at the ceiling, which was pulsating. It started to glisten. "Aren't you happy yet?" she said, turning toward me, her best friend.

"Yeah, sometimes." My organs were sinking inside my body and my face was getting hot. My fingers began tingling. A confusing flush washed over me. This was a side effect of the cough syrup. Maybe, though, I was in love with the boy singing on the computer. Or maybe it was Candy. It was, I thought, as she put her hand on my cheek and kissed me, deeply. It was my first kiss, and she knew that. I kissed her back and felt everything everyone had said would happen. Fireworks, lightheadedness, shuddering warmth, all of it different than what I'd imagined. We wrapped our arms around each other and kissed until Candy broke the silence, which was eventually weighing us down.

"We should save some for later," and then, "That was fun, though, right? Are you happy now?"

"Yes," I said, smiling. But a piece of what she had said was painful. "What do you mean?"

"Nothing, god." And it was done. We had to eat something to level out, even though the cough syrup killed our appetites completely.

Norma would hate Candy, I could tell. I had started to worry about that when someone buzzed the apartment. "I'll be right down," I said into the wall.

"I'll come up, don't be silly," Norma said back. One second later, like a slow blink, my aunt was knocking on the door. Candy looked at me like it was my fault. I opened it and blocked the entry-way with my body.

"I'm ready. We can go."

"Hi, I'm Norma." She shoved past me.

Candy laughed. "I know who you are." She laughed again in a higher pitch. "I waved at you from the car at school."

Norma looked at me. It was the first time I'd seen her appear nervous. "What are your plans for the day?"

Candy waited for the silence to sharpen. "I'm hanging out with my boyfriend," she said, still looking at me. I wanted to leave, then, but not to go home, to Norma's home. The carpeted floor was cauliflowering.

The start of Candy and Robert's relationship was explained to me as something beyond romantic: they each liked one another, but their shyness prevented one from letting the other know. Robert was seventeen, the same age as Candy's sister. He had a car but was a loner in school. Outside of school, he hung out with kids who had graduated or dropped out.

Candy was different from the girls Robert knew. She didn't care about vampires or makeup, but she knew about the *Faces of Death* VHS tapes you couldn't find in the library or at Blockbuster. She was a vegetarian and loved looking at the potted plants at Home Depot, dreaming of the day she would have a yard. One night, outside of the Liquid Room, Candy said hello to Robert. How did she know about the band that was about to play? Candy knew about every local band. She checked message boards and weeklies and venue calendars and researched names, making lists of the music she liked and writing down the all-ages shows in her own personal planner. She loved this band, she told Robert, in front of the girls with black lipstick, who were just there to be there, which was obvious because they weren't paying the cover. He smiled, and then they went inside together. While the music played and they looked straight ahead at the stage, Robert felt for Candy's hand and held it.

I could imagine a boy saving my life. I'd suffered, it felt, a disproportionate amount, and boys seemed to want to deal with that. No boys had ever asked me out, though. Neither had they ever tried to hold my hand. I had never gotten a call from one of the boys in my classes, who all had my number since kindergarten because it was listed in the school directory. My friends back in Ypsi had made excuses for me. I was too tall, or too intimidating, or too quiet, they said. I should play sports, they said. And then I moved to Grand Rapids, and I didn't join any sports, and the boys at my new school didn't seem to like me, either. Maybe everyone was right.

I sat in my basement room reading paperbacks Norma had kept since college and staring out the narrow window into the dark woods. I imagined something happening to me, anything, to shock me back into my brain. In one book I read, a group of men found a body in the river. They carried on, discussing what to do next with their disrupted lives. When I got to the end, I felt I'd missed something. What had happened to the body?

It was my turn to show Candy something, I thought. She'd been showing me so many movies and songs and things I would never forget, things I was embarrassed to love instantly in front of her. Her mix CDs had no songs I'd heard on the radio. They made me wonder if all I had ever experienced before was one layer of many. All I could offer Candy was stories about what it was like in Ypsi. She wanted to know everything. So, I showed her my message history with the politician. She was more intrigued by the friend with whom I'd started the conversation.

"Gina," I said. "We don't talk anymore."

"Why not?"

She wasn't my closest friend, I explained, and once I thought about it, it was strange she was ever at my house at all. I was abstractly pained, attempting to remember the circumstances that would lead to such a casual friendship, a sleepover with a schoolmate for no reason, with my mother making popcorn in the kitchen so we could watch a TV movie under the heavy yellow blanket that was thinning along its quilting. "You know how you just had anyone from your class over, back then?"

"No," said Candy, fixated on the screen. "I never did that. Once, but that was Lauren. She basically begged me if she could come over."

"Why don't you like Lauren?" I asked, pulled into the present.

"She just sucks and I just really, really, hate how much she sucks. And she sucked in fourth grade, when she slept over. She woke up early and asked my dad to make her pancakes. And he didn't have pancake mix, and she was like, *Why not?* She's just always asking these stupid questions, being so annoying."

I'd loved sleepovers. All of them. Phone calls with my old friends were getting shorter and shorter. Everyone got called to dinner earlier and earlier. New names were emerging in stories, and it was harder for me to keep up. "Should we message the politician?" I asked Candy.

"Yeah, but let me do it," she said.

"I have to say I saw him on *Grosse Income*," I said. "I haven't told him yet."

"No, you don't," said Candy. "He probably wouldn't like that."

Every day, I would watch the reruns, hoping to spot him again. Grosse Pointe looked prettier than Grand Rapids. It had bars and restaurants lit with tomato-red neon, montages of jazz bands playing for a room with a curved ceiling, a bridge dotted with light that reflected onto the purple Detroit River.

A younger man, younger than the residents, but still old, came into the dining room. He wore a close fitting knit cap, but I could tell he was bald. He introduced himself to me and I immediately forgot his name.

"You're new," he told me. "I visit my father here often." He opened the flap of a leather messenger bag, exposing three VHS cassettes, movies his dad liked to watch with him. They were all recorded from television, their white sticker labels scrawled with unreadable handwriting. As he spoke, the man's voice became distant, like a radio, and I remembered a pill I took with my Prozac. It was something Candy got from her mom, a prescription, but not one of her Xanax. Maybe this pill was nothing. So many pills are.

"It might seem out of nowhere," the man said, "but I have to ask, since this is the way I always work. Would you like to be in my movie? I'm a filmmaker."

Without hesitation, I agreed to let him pick me up after my shift.

"Bertha Gillins needs a blanket for her legs," said the shift manager. I went to the hall closet to fetch a shriveled and pilled little pile. Bertha, Ernest, Margaret, Dorothea, Douglas, Francesca, Rosemary—all the names, typed on ignored place cards in little square formations in the middle of each round table, sounded either too cheerful or too dignified to describe any of these people.

Everyone had a nickname. Lorna was called Lonny, Theodora was Teddy, Henrietta was Ricky. These sounded more appropriately babyish, especially while the residents were being fed their luke-warm cereals with rubber-coated spoons. We called some by their last names only. Mrs. Ducote insisted on being called Mrs. Ducote. Her husband was dead, but she talked about "Mr. Ducote" as if he was not. She was white-haired and delicate, and the RNs said that she was anorexic because she wanted attention.

Anne Morris, who we always called by her first and last name for some reason, wore tortoiseshell sunglasses when she got visits. When her grandchildren, a boy and a girl, came to take her out, she probably complained to them, but when they didn't, she complained to us. Anne Morris and Mary Schaffer were the only residents with red hair. They were also two out of the three residents with any hair color at all, though Lonny Weller didn't really count. Her jet-black wig looked like a newsboy cap. It would probably fall into her food if she were able to move her neck.

This was before I moved back to Ypsi, reconnected with some friends, ran into people I had forgotten existed, like my old teachers and my mom's old friends, at the grocery store or the movie theater.

The way women grow up is into each other. The people that stay in Grand Rapids spend money to sit. They check themselves in for hours at a salon to come out tinted and striped, their eyes whiter against the tans and highlights, whereas the East Michiganders I know mostly do their moping at bars. Everyone is watching TV the whole time, and I'm the same, don't get me wrong. You said you don't like TV. I don't either. But I do watch it. If I'm being honest, I watch a lot of it. This conversation is starting to get tedious, and that's my fault. But it's also yours.

The more I speak with people I knew from that time, the more the past becomes opaque. Everyone turned into their parents, and I became some random person. Candy's life is predictable from the outside, but whenever we speak, which is rarely, her voice sounds sped up, not true to my memory of her. I am exactly the same, everyone says of me, as if that's a compliment.

I used to look at each of the residents at Berrylawn and wonder which one we would turn out most like, which one was Candy, which one was me. On certain days, Candy was Genie Kemp, with her pleading, tiny hands. The way she turned to face something with her whole body, squirming in her wheelchair, the way she bounced attention off herself. I was Millie or Helen, quietly staring in Genie or Anne's direction, watching the silent television, forgetting where she was.

The filmmaker was leaning on an old white station wagon when I opened the back door to the parking lot. "Tess," he yelled, as if I wasn't walking toward him. I stood, listening, while he talked about girls who wanted to be in his movies but didn't want to get into his car. I got into his car. As he drove out of the lot and down the street in the direction opposite my aunt and uncle's house, I tried to sort out the soggy feeling in my head. My teeth were floating in my mouth, and I faintly needed to pee. I became confused by all the references to this guy's "girlfriend," his "ex-girlfriend," his "girlfriend's new boyfriend," and the "girl that slept with" him and his girlfriend, the one that also would not be in his movie and was "kind of a bitch."

We arrived at an abandoned building. There were no doors in the frames anymore. Everything happened quickly, the dusty light swinging past us as we stepped over cinder blocks filled with ash and plastic buckets filled with a hardened liquid. I kept imagining how embarrassing it would be if I tripped over some detritus and fell on my knees. I wondered if I would be able to handle it if I saw my own blood. I'd never been in a theater class, but the emotions came easily, at least according to this man. He filmed me yelling a monologue he'd written on a folded white page and held in front of me while also holding a camera. We were in what looked like a bombed-out classroom, in front of a large window overlooking the destruction of another school-like building.

As he was packing up his camera after we finished the scene, he told me I could see one of his finished films if I'd like. Instinctively,

I said I had to go home. Maybe another time. I wrote my aunt and uncle's phone number on a fresh piece of notebook paper, and he wrote my name next to it as fast as if he were signing his own. He shut the notebook and slid it into the messenger bag on the ground, trying to look official while his body was bent in half.

Later, in my diary, I would list this man as one of the many who disappointed me.

Growing up in Ypsilanti felt like nothing until I moved away, and then all the little differences created the city for me. It felt flatter, or maybe that was just our street, and dirtier, in a lively way. There were more people walking around. There were students from EMU everywhere, dressed as one of a few types of hippie or athlete.

To my classmates in Grand Rapids, I filled out my own perception of Ypsi: weed was basically legal there and I used to see it sold all over the place; during Hash Bash, clouds of smoke would hover over the city for a week. I was a full-on stoner back then, I'd say, unhappy with the lack of substances in my new school. The exaggerations became my personal reality. I had nothing in common with the kids around me, that was true. I didn't miss my dad, not really. Or I'd already gotten past missing him. I did miss my old friends, but only until I met Candy. I had thought that the way to be cool was to show the least amount of effort possible, but Candy, the coolest person I'd ever met, did everything, and looked down on anyone who didn't.

"You should have black hair, like PJ Harvey."

"Who's that?" I asked, staring at the ceiling and slowly spinning in a circle before collapsing. The room kept turning in staccato motion, like a grunge music video.

"Are you kidding? Cassie! Cassie!" Candy's sister eventually came into the room. I was burying my face in a stuffed rabbit.

"You guys," Cassie said. "Should I be worried right now?"

"Yes," exclaimed Candy. "Tess doesn't know who PJ Harvey is."

"What?" said Cassie. "You need to. You need to right now. I'm going to go put it on in the living room. Come out when you're ready."

I wanted Cassie to pick me up, to carry me out. That would be so fun, to get a piggyback ride. The music came on and it sounded like it was coming from headphones wrapped in a paper bag, but also like it was echoing inside of me.

"Cassie, no, you have to start it over." Candy was running from one corner of their bedroom to the other, tripping over my limp body and falling over the pillows. I stretched to grab her by the ankle, but she was ripping dresses down from hangers in the closet. She found a dark blue satin slip. She never wore underwear and always changed in front of anyone who happened to be around, not holding a shirt over her nipples or putting one skirt over another before pulling it down. Her body was muscly, pale, freckled and veined. It didn't look good in the clothes she chose to wear, but naked, she was a classic beauty. The blue slip clung to her hips and was loose everywhere else, the straps falling, one and then the other. "Come on, get up," she said, wide-eyed. I did, and followed her, my head bouncing on the spring of my neck with each step. "Start it over, start it over, please, Cassie, come on." We were in the living room.

"Okay, Jesus, I am." Cassie hit the back button on the CD player, which was part of a huge system that connected a big screen TV and Blu-ray player to giant speakers in opposite corners. Candy was in the center of the floor, crouched, her head between her knees, her palms flat, perfectly still. Cassie corralled me onto the leather couch, sitting close. Outside, a car passed the building and flooded the room with white light that bloomed on my eyes. As I looked at Candy's body, a ball in the middle of a carpeted floor, silent and faceless, the thought crossed my mind that she would one day die.

The music started, a one-note bass line and a soft, flaky snare drum that I assumed was my own heartbeat. When the female voice started whispering, "Tie yourself to me, no one else, no," I assumed it was Candy. I'd expected PJ Harvey to be a man. She stood up one vertebra at a time, facing away from us. One leg crossed behind the other and spun her in our direction. She was breathing heavily on the right syllables, snaking her shoulders. Her hands rose to her face, cradling a trembling mouth. "I'll make you lick my injuries, I'm gonna twist your head off, see."

The guitar came crashing in so loud that I jumped, and her arms came crashing down, her hands now fists pounding her hips. I had never seen anyone lip synch the way you're supposed to do it, like this. The song got quiet again, whimpering, "I beg you, my darling, don't leave me, I'm hurting," and soon it got loud again, for longer this time. Her slip fell and exposed a nipple. Cassie got up and reached to fix it, but Candy was shaking her head and bending down as if she really was screaming and soon the whole slip shimmied, so the top was at her waist. For the last quiet verse, she kneeled on the carpet, looking up as if in prayer.

The RNs were always telling Cal, short for Caledonia, to sit up straighter when she was fed and to stop throwing her things on the floor. Sometimes she carried a soft leather purse, which she stuffed with tissues, her collectable thimbles, and a comb that looked like it was made of pearl.

I almost envied Cal as she slouched and resisted like a baby. I pictured Norma shoving me toward the car, insisting I go to church, and me, flinging my purse onto the garage floor, slumping into the corner behind cardboard boxes and the wet vac, refusing to say a word or make eye contact until the family took off, leaving me alone for the morning.

Standing in the hallway after leaving the steamy kitchen, catching my breath, I sensed someone rolling up behind me.

"What are you doing?" asked Anne Morris, dragging out each vowel.

"I was just making coffee."

"Well, I think I'd like to watch you do that."

"I've already finished."

"I gotta find something to do. I gotta get cleaned up and go to my folks' place, which is a long way away. I can't see straight."

"I'm sure there's something to do in the activities room," I said, although I wasn't sure of that. I knew there were volunteer girls who taught aerobics there sometimes, which included turning the head from side to side, slowly, again, slowly, again. I left my station and pushed Anne Morris to the end of the hall, but the activities room was locked.

"Sometimes I think I should jump in the lake and get it over with," she said.

"What lake?"

"Sometimes I think I should come out here and just cut my throat in front of everyone."

"Don't do that," I said in an Equal-packet voice. I hated myself for being so phony with any of them, but all the RNs smiled at the residents' suicide threats after a while. They weren't real threats, with all the monitors and restraints set up there, and cheerfulness was the only type of response that could cut the conversation short. Anne Morris started wailing, telling me that I didn't know how awful it was for her. She was right, but she didn't know eggs from toast. I turned back towards the kitchen, and she stopped crying. "I think I'll walk around some," she said, and then added, "in my wheelchair." She rolled away from me, using her feet to crawl.

I retied my apron and buttoned my tuxedo shirt to the throat. The line cook was in the kitchen prepping for breakfast. Neither of us spoke. I watched the little glass pudding cups being filled with perfect swirls of yellow and brown from a spouted bag and then took the tray to my station. Following a laminated layout of the dining room with dietary restrictions written on each place, I left cups in front of the cards of the residents that were allowed to have pudding. The residents filed in, pushed by nurses. It was still early. Their faces were like mountains as seen from a plane, shadowed by little clouds.

Genie was known to take out her dentures at the table. She was also known to hoard trash and try to eat it with her gaping toothless mouth after breakfast was over. I'd seen her try to trip other wheelchairs with a slippered foot and get pushed aside. Her frame was so tiny, she must have either been a small woman her whole life or be suffering some illness that made her bones wear away.

My mother had shrunk when she was sick. She'd gone from being taller to shorter than me, before she was bedridden. Marge dropped her plate on the floor and stared off while Anne Morris sobbed like a child who'd forgotten what she was crying about.

Genie was relatively quiet that morning, meaning she didn't try to get up out of her wheelchair. If she did, a magnet that attached the back of her shirt to the front of the chair would sound an alarm, signaling an escape attempt. Only a few wheelchairs had alarms. For some, they worked like shock collars, scaring the residents into sitting still. For others, they were a way to change the mood of the room.

When school was in session, Candy had listed her favorite summer activities, like Blues on the Mall downtown and the Lowell fair. She had always wanted to go to the World's Largest Antique Store and to see the fish ladder. Grand Rapids was only fun in the summer, she said, when you can go out in the streets and meet new people.

The first day of summer break, though, Candy had to go to Lansing to visit her grandparents. I forgot and tried to call her, but the phone just kept ringing. I wandered out of my room. The house was quiet. The basement TV room was usually taken over by the boys, peeling off hockey or football gear, watching football or hockey while Norma was watching something else in the living room. It was empty this morning.

Norma and John were out shopping for a gift before attending a birthday party for a baby. My cousins were probably at some kind of practice or youth group or pool party, maybe a combination of all three. Norma usually made a later breakfast on Saturdays just for "us girls," a healthier meal of fruit and granola. She'd set it on the table for me and say things like, "It's okay, sleeping in is good for you once in a while."

Flipping channels, I usually ended up pausing for longest on the Home Shopping Network. Something was slowly rotating, cut metal gleaming on a mirror-plated rack. If Sheila were alive, she would say I was wasting a nice day. I had never been this alone in my short little life so far, I thought. I kept a vintage pill planner on my nightstand, an enameled metal tray of seven plastic drawers, even though the dose I took every day was the same. I swallowed one Prozac capsule without water.

Sunlight sifted in through the basement's half-windows like the drawings of biblical prisoners in some coloring book or worksheet. What parties would I miss tonight, not having been seen by those who were throwing them? How many joyrides would I be offered if I was sitting in some parking lot, instead of here? What drugs would older kids have given me just to see a girl experience something for the first time?

Lauren was my first friend in Grand Rapids. The day I met her, she wore a polyester zip-up printed with a pattern of sexy girl silhouettes and shoes with fat blue laces stamped with pink cartoon mushrooms. She bought everything at a store downtown that my uncle called "the head shop," where he sometimes picked up an expensive chewing tobacco. Lauren's boyfriend's hair was bleached and starting to dread. Hers was a faded purple. In our art class, she refused to complete the drawing assignment because it felt too "prescriptive."

My hair was the color of dead grass then; my washed black polo shirt had no insignia and was gummy with sweat in the pits, and yet Lauren's first words to me were, "You look cool." I was drawing a vase of sunflowers from life. I looked up, imagining some overweight nervous girl who had failed to make friends the year before attempting again with a new kid. Instead, I saw Lauren's heart shaped face and sleepy eyes. Her skin looked like beach sand, almost shimmering.

I had seen Lauren walking around outside with her boyfriend during lunch hour, picking dandelions and stuffing them behind his ears. Still, I wondered if she was coming on to me. It was the way she kept doubling over the desk and then looking at me sideways. She sat in the chair next to mine and talked about nothing for a whole class period. Her parents wanted her to go with them on a vacation this summer to SeaWorld, as if she was still a little kid. Her grandmother was in the hospital, and it was making her whole family crazy. She had just got tickets to this rave in Detroit that night and her boyfriend couldn't go anymore. She invited me, about an hour after meeting me. I'd said I couldn't because I had a curfew, but the reality was I didn't believe her. The next day, in class, she said it was good we hadn't gone, since the rave got raided.

I climbed the basement stairs into the big empty house and searched the fridge. There was no reason not to call Lauren, other than I never had before. Her number was written in my school planner. A woman that sounded very old answered and I thought, for a queasy second, she may have tricked me. "Is Lauren there?"

"Yes, in fact she is. I'll get her."

"Hey, I just got my car back." Lauren's voice drifted in and out as she explained what had needing fixing, as if I'd known her car was in the shop, or that she had a car. I told her my address and she said she knew where it was, that it would take her twenty minutes. I got dressed and walked to the end of the driveway and waited. Across the street, a bird was carrying pieces of straw from a bail meant to be used as a bench, one by one, to a secret place in the trees.

When Lauren drove up, smoking a cigarette out the window, the bird dropped what was in its beak and became a dot in the sky. The car stereo was playing fast punk rock I didn't recognize. Lauren's hair had been gelled into flattened tufts, calligraphic gestures forming a blondish crown still streaked with hints of violet. I had seen her in school only days ago, wearing a snap bead necklace hung with a double cherry air freshener, at which Candy had rolled her eyes and said, "It's like she's making fun of herself." Today, she wore a spiked dog collar. I asked if it was from the head shop.

"No, the pet store," said Lauren. "You like it?"

I did. And I liked her car, a yellow VW Karmann Ghia.

I was supposed to have met Candy first. She approached me after a pep rally, holding Robert's hand, dragging him along as she caught up to me. "Wasn't that stupid?" she asked.

Robert said, "Obviously," and then Candy pulled her hand out of his and thrust it at me. "Are you new here?"

"You know she is," said Robert.

"Where are you from?"

"Ypsilanti," I said. Candy was pretty, but it was clear she hadn't accepted this. Her steps were like a small dog's. Her head moved quickly, too, making it difficult to make eye contact with her. She looked back and forth between Robert and I, like one of us should do the talking.

"I'm from Lansing," she said, "originally." Her dress shifted as she swung her arms too fast, exposing a large enough window of skin to confirm that she was not wearing a bra. Her whole body was dusted with freckles and her skin was so pale it shone bluish on her wrists and sternum. Her favorite dress, the one she was wearing when we met, was made of white and metallic thread. It was too big and had been washed too many times. It apparently had no nostalgic or special value; it was just a dress that didn't give her away as uninterested in fashion. She wore no jewelry, no nail polish. Even shoelaces were too busy for her. She wore patent leather boots that zipped up the sides. She'd bought them at a thrift shop and didn't know what brand they were. Robert wore combat boots with eighteen eyeholes. He bought all his clothing from the army surplus store.

I saw Candy again in the hallway the next day. She asked me where I lived. I told her my aunt and uncle's address, since I couldn't say much more about the area. She laughed and ran away, disappearing into a classroom. That Sunday, when John and Norma and the cousins and I were returning from church, there was a CD jewel case on the doorstep. It said, in permanent marker, "For Tess," inside of a heart. Everyone made a huge deal about me having a secret admirer, and then I opened the case to find a handwritten playlist on a torn piece of paper marked with the words, "From Candy."

"Who?" asked John.

"A girl in my school," I said, blushing.

No one said anything. I went down to my room.

When I send Candy that PJ Harvey song now, in a text, she remembers it being a favorite of hers, but not its significance to me, or to us. When I hear it, I am reminded of her, of the newness of drugs, of an orgasm I had yet to experience, of a time when listening to music, even, was novel.

Everything dulls, though, and CDs scratch, inkjet printouts blister with moisture, a cutout's edges soften, memories become just that. What made her dynamic then, to me, becomes indescribable now, even to myself, because it is tethered to a time, and that time looks different when it is a pile of cracked plastic jewel cases in a battered shoebox. Still, I like the song, and probably wouldn't even get to feel that if not for some earlier enjoyment of it. I can't remember what was always playing in Lauren's car, which is funny, because eventually, I remember, I complained about the repetition.

Lauren's house was in one suburb and mine was in another. Everyone at our school was bussed in from what Candy called McMansions in all the neighboring areas, but no one came from downtown, where we were headed.

The coffee shop was called Tate's—it said so on the awning—but everyone only called it "the coffee shop," meaning the only one that was open 24 hours. Lauren parked in a dirt lot behind the strip of storefronts. It was humid and my pollen allergies were awake. Inside, though, the air was dry with cigarette smoke and textured with the sounds of a cappuccino machine and a dishwasher. Our boots tracked dried mud onto a reddish hardwood floor that was blackened in the entryway, near the counter, and outside the bathroom. A chalkboard said that today's specials were a Smashing Pumpkin Latte and a Pearl Jam Danish. I pointed to the decorated text, but Lauren told me not to order either, that everyone just got black coffee. It was true: the two people sitting at separate little tables were drinking from thrifted promotional mugs, smoking behind paperback books.

Lauren said hello to the guy behind the counter. "Like my new look?" she asked. She swiveled, one hand on her hip, showing him black jeans so tight they had to have been cut and re-sewn to fit her. The guy, who wore a polo shirt and thin suspenders, did not appear to recognize her. He nodded, whatever. He was cute, I realized. Or he was nothing like anyone in our school. He was older than us but different in other ways, too. I blushed as I ordered a black coffee and he handed me an empty mug to self-serve from a selection of three roasts.

"I come here every day before school," said Lauren, at a table.

"How do you get up that early?"

"I just can't go to school without coffee. I'm like, dead."

"I would not be able to drive all the way here and then back to school," I countered. I also didn't have a car, or a license. Lauren was a year older than the rest of our class, because, she said, she got held back in kindergarten. We sat at a small table on a raised area that looked like a stage. I peered around us and out the window at passersby. We could be invited to a party, maybe. There were parties always happening, here or in a neighboring town, I was positive: bonfires, house parties, all-ages clubs. The summer before was when Sheila and I moved to Grand Rapids, and we'd spent that one looking for jobs and, in my case, finding one. A man turned a page in his book and stubbed out a cigarette while lighting another. I told Lauren the plan I'd made with Candy, that we were supposed to spend every day together this summer.

"Looks like you're blowing the plan."

"It starts after the weekend."

"I don't think Candy likes me," said Lauren. "I don't know why, though. We used to be friends in like, second grade."

I didn't smoke but I was smoking one of Lauren's cigarettes. I thought I might puke and walked to the bathroom, where I locked myself in and put my head between my knees while I peed and farted. I flushed and drank some water from the faucet. I breathed deeply in the little stall, full of graffitied poetry and local band stickers. A flyer advertised an open mic night. There was an entire society of people who didn't have to go to school or work and could spend their lives reading books and magazines. If I stayed in the bathroom long enough, Lauren was going to say something about how long I took. When I opened the door, one of the two other people there was standing and waiting, his book still in his hand.

"Should we go?" Lauren shouted while I crossed the room.

I waited until I was sitting down again to answer. "Go where?"

"I'm gonna call my friend who always knows." Lauren produced a cell phone from her purse. Her parents bought it for her, she explained, because she rarely came home, and they were always trying to reach her. She pressed an arrow-shaped button many times, searching for someone's contact.

"What about your boyfriend?"

"We broke up."

"Oh."

"That was so long ago." Lauren's expression grew distant for the first time.

Just as a deep-voiced song started to play, the front door opened, and a man with black hair, probably dyed, and eyes cornered with liner came in. When he walked, it sounded like spurs announcing the stranger coming to town in a Western because there were chains wrapped around each heel of his motorcycle boots. He was thin and tall but hunched over, reaching ahead of himself with long arms.

"I need, I need," he said, before the guy behind the counter put a mug in his hand. "Better make it one of them disposable ones." He grabbed a paper cup from a stack himself. He filled it quickly and tried to drink the hot coffee like it was water, then howled, his tongue apparently burned. He never reached for a wallet but pretended to tip a hat, and then said, "Fuck me," turning around and stumbling out the door again. The guy in suspenders chuckled to himself and picked up a rag to wipe his counter.

"Do you know him?" Lauren knew that I didn't. "Stephen. He's here a lot."

Outside, Stephen was talking to two other people with blue-black hair, maybe a couple. He walked in the other direction as soon as we started for the parking lot. Lauren asked if I wanted to play Cherry Bomb with her cigarette butt. It was when you put the still-lit cherry on your forearm and the other person presses theirs against it, too, she explained. Whoever jumps back first loses. I didn't want to, but more than that I didn't want to say I didn't want to, so I stuck my arm out. The couple stood against the wall to watch us as Lauren pressed the burning ash to the inside of her shimmery-smooth arm, sucking through her teeth and saying, "Hurry, do it."

The burn was like a jab, so hot it was cold and sharp, and then a twisting pinch. I saw white for an instant. Our arms were still touching, but the butt had fallen to the ground.

"You pulled away," she said.

"No, I didn't."

"Someone lose a bet?" asked one of the strangers.

The burn had introduced an unfamiliar adrenaline. We got back into Lauren's car and looked at our blistering wounds. "What should I do to hide it from my aunt and uncle?"

"I have a bunch of clothes in the trunk. Borrow something with long sleeves. Didn't you say you have to do something today?"

"Yeah, I gotta go to work. Shit."

After the tables were cleared, the dish washer would have to sort the cups and plates and silverware from the bins into the racks he fed into an industrial machine, then set the hot utensils aside to dry before I could put them away. If I reached for them, he would put his hand in front of the rack, wordlessly signaling that they were not cool enough to touch yet. The dish washer and I didn't speak. Once, I told him that we were wearing the same shoes, and then I looked down and realized we were not, that I hadn't worn my sneakers that day. I wasn't even allowed to wear sneakers to work, since it wasn't part of the uniform. Instead of explaining, I laughed, pretending it was a joke he didn't understand.

I broke a sweat moving around the spray of hot water, the burn on my arm throbbing, squeezed by the steam. When I was finished taking the dishes to their metal cabinets, I snuck into the walk-in freezer and held it against a tub of ice cream, letting the cold seep through my sleeve. I replayed the whole trip to the coffee shop in my head, stopping on Stephen, his eyeliner, his hangover. I imagined what Stephen had done the night before, what he was doing now, what he would do later.

When it was time to, I clocked out and walked home. I always told myself I would take a different route, and then I would see the shortest distance and walk it. I trudged up the driveway and through the garage door, down the basement stairs. I sat on the couch there, watching my cousins watch an action movie and pretending to care about it while the image of Stephen was suspended above me, reaching for coffee. Were they cowboy or combat boots he was wearing? I started to forget his face except for the squinting eyes.

"Do you want to watch something else?" asked Justin, the older one. He was looking at me, I realized, remote outstretched in my direction.

"No, I don't care," I said. "I mean, this is cool."

It was exhausting, never being able to melt the tension of knowing that people were pitying me. Even if my cousins were my cousins, they were boys, and next year one would be in my school, probably more popular than me, even with the juniors, since he played football. My body ticked while I lay on the couch. A fold of fat settled around my belly button when I curled up. I put my hand under my shirt and held it.

This is the scar from the cigarette. It's barely there now, but you can see it. Embarrassing. What's wild is that no one, not my aunt or uncle or cousins or therapist, asked me about it. And I'm sure they noticed, because it blistered.

Later, my dad asked me about it, though. That means nothing to you because you don't know me, but just as a reference, I used to steal my dad's car at night, when I lived with him again, and he either didn't know or didn't say anything. Sometimes I'd just drive in a loop. I was always scared of running out of gas because I'd never pumped it and thought that would be impossible to figure out alone.

Oh, I just told him it was from cooking eggs. The grease jumped out and burned me. Do you have any scars?

I had hardly been to a church when my mother was alive, and now I had to go every Sunday, first thing in the morning. Norma and John seemed to genuinely love it, and even the boys seemed to like it because it was "the cool church." There was a group that they called a rock band, with a Plexiglas partition in front of the drum set so it wouldn't be too loud. During services, projected slideshows and videos diagrammed what happiness and devotion was supposed to look like.

I learned almost nothing about the Bible and its characters. They were mentioned and quoted, but always in that way that assumed we had heard this all before. We were told to remember the gospel of whoever when thinking about a present-day situation, like a crisis of faith in the family. On the wall, we could focus on stock images of houses and dollar signs, cartoon families that looked a lot like mine, without me.

Almost every time I went to this church, some boy my cousins knew would introduce himself to me. Then I would have to think of myself as a girl talking to a boy, no matter how young or unattractive or ambivalent he was.

"Pleasure to meet you." I would feel the hot flames of embarrassment licking my face. This place, its shiny white walls, its taupe carpeting, and its polyester flags, got weirder every week. At first, I wore my plaid skirts, black tights, and buttoned shirts, at least nodding to the formality associated with the other times I'd been to churches: for a Christmas pageant, a wedding, a funeral. Soon, though, I understood that part of being the cool church was a casual dress code. Men wore what they would on a job site, putting wraparound sunglasses on the backs of their heads during service. Women wore buttoned shirts and jeans, boots, or clogs with a slight heel. The acoustics made everything sound like it was coming from a foam-covered speaker.

In the corners of my eyes, boys tapped their feet to the band. I let my vision blur. Outside in the parking lot, things could be different: they were older, taller, darker, smelling like sweat from the sun's heat. They were smiling because one day they would yank the sad electric guitar from its owner's long, boney hands and smash it into the sound barricade until they both splintered. They would nod sideways to me as they stormed out, recognizing that I was lost there and needed finding, letting me jump onto the handlebars of a bike or the front of a skateboard or the bench seat of a convertible.

In my fantasies, it was always a group of guys taking me off to a party or a diner, sitting in the smoking section, and it was always a rowdy conversation, the sounds distorting the focus as the one and only runaway girl in the center grew crisp. That was what I could offer, if not interesting anecdotes or sexual prowess: I would leave everything behind if given the chance. Not everyone would do that. I'd already left behind so much without having been asked.

Since Sheila was diagnosed, I was the inconsolable child, the piously loving daughter, the hardened early adult, the inconsiderate kid, the diagnosed depressed teenager, the medicated person. Even before the medication, though, I started to feel and see things like the symptoms of nervous disorders. Sometimes my peripheral vision would go white or streaked with red, and I had to find a bathroom in the hospital that didn't have stalls so I could lie down on a cold floor.

When Sheila finally died, after her flesh sunk around her bones, which were also disintegrating but slower, I was gripped by a relatively more tangible pain, which was somewhat grounding. I was either there or not, not in between. I explained all of this carefully to my therapist, who, I decided, was not really listening. "It's hard to find a good therapist," someone said in a TV show I was watching. Mine was free with Medicaid. She gave me my prescription after one visit.

I was already high all the time but getting higher offered a spectrum of brighter experiences, a piece of glass held up to a drifting beam of light. A feeling came and went, and when it was gone, I missed it, but when it was back, it scared me. The idea that feelings could return scared me. I spent whole days in bed, staring at patterns the sun made on my door, dust particles floating through them. I thought, hopefully, that I was going insane.

There were ways to be good, the pastor said. You could be good at something, you could follow the rules, and you could be, in your very being, good. There was something deep inside, that you would have to find for yourself and work on. There is a flame burning in each of us that is our goodness that God gave us, and it is our job to tend to it. Don't let it go out. Make it a roaring, glorious fire with which everyone can share the warmth.

Afterwards, we would usually go grocery shopping, and I would slip a bottle or two of Robitussin into my purse, for later. After these rituals, there would be more: a big lunch at home and then sports on TV in the living room. I'd go back to my basement bedroom and turn up my music so loud that John would knock on my door, ready to yell at me, but, met with red eyes and mussed hair, he'd meekly ask if I could turn it down a couple notches so they could hear the game. I was welcome to join if I wanted.

When my room felt like a mouth, I went upstairs to use the computer in the office. After an hour or two, I stood up from the desk chair and noticed I had bled on its tweedy fabric. In the master bathroom, which was the closest to the office, I looked for something to clean up the stain. It felt cruel that period blood kept showing up, even when I felt so outside of myself. How did drug addicts deal with something this bodily? What would it be like once I was an adult, at a bar all the time, looking down at blood that I would have to clean up while trying to appear fun?

Sheila had told me, before she was sick, that a period is basically always a mess. She couldn't remember a time when she'd not gotten blood on something at least once a month, and she'd been dealing with it for decades. At the time, it sounded unbelievable and sad. Now, it was believable, and sad in another way.

I first looked through Norma's cabinets. Years of lipstick and mascara tubes in plastic baskets, near-empty perfume bottles, cans of air freshener, wrapped soaps, expired credit cards, contact lens solution, miniature Ziplocs of buttons, a filmy grocery bag filled with "conditioning shampoo" bottles from hotels, light bulbs small enough to replace the ones on the professional makeup mirror, sewing kits, first aid kits, lice shampoo, calcium-crusted travel manicure kits hemmed with plastic thread, unopened eye shadow palettes, plastic-bristled hairbrushes and plastic-toothed combs, waxed floss, crumbling beet juice plaque tablets and Alka-Seltzer in unmarked wrappers, gobs of sticky substances the color of earwax that had leaked from something now missing, and a cardboard carton of Epsom salt disintegrating into itself, but no tampons or pads. Not even any panty liners. Back behind all of that was a small, spiral-bound notebook as thick as a novel.

Sitting on the toilet, I opened it and read the first page: *December 4, 1995. What a thoughtful gift, from my sister. I've never written in a diary before, if you can believe that. This already feels strange. Well, we'll see where it goes.* We'll see where it goes, and then nothing, the end of the first entry.

I stuffed a wad of toilet paper into the hammock of my underwear. My thumb caught a drop of perfectly consistent blood. I could hear dinner settings being arranged downstairs. I closed the diary, unintentionally marking the first page with a red fingerprint, which darkened to rust. Someone was calling out, making a sound that could be my name. I put the book back in its hiding place. I forgot about the stained chair. The next time I looked at it, someone had rubbed it with detergent, which lightened the stain but darkened the area around it.

"We always went to Big Sky when you lived here," said Keri, on the phone. "You don't remember?"

"No," I said.

"It's the diner, on Washtenaw," she insisted.

"I would remember if I'd gone there."

"It's the best," said Keri, her voice far away. "Wait, did we tell you about Jake? I mean, do you know about Jake? That he's gay now?"

"No. Jake?"

"From our school. He's the best. You remember Jake."

None of these places or people had existed before, except they had, apparently, in my own life. My mother had a friend, a gay man, and I felt like bringing this up. But we were not friends, and she was not alive, so he was just a man, living his own life somewhere.

"He had a pool party, and everyone came, and it was pretty much him telling us all about his new life and that gay people have way more fun, and I believe him."

Keri was talking to someone else in the room, I could tell, but she didn't put them on the phone, or say who it was. "Is Gina there?" I asked, and the line went quiet.

"Why?" asked Keri.

I'd said something wrong. There was no recovering.

"I gotta go," she shouted, not waiting for me to say goodbye before hanging up.

The first Sunday of summer break was the premiere of *Grosse Income*'s second season. On trailers, it described itself as "a reality show about the wealthy and the washed up in one of the richest suburbs in America." Everyone was going to watch it, even Norma and John, who had not seen the first season, but had heard enough about it to throw their arms up in surrender. "We'll have to check it out," Norma always said after one of her friends at the grocery store talked about the most recent episode with breathy enthusiasm.

Norma usually didn't allow television at dinner, but would make an exception for this premiere, much to the confusion of my cousins. Who cared about Grosse Pointe? they asked. It may as well be in Canada.

"West Michigan is the dead zone," I argued.

"Hey, hey," said John.

Everyone we knew had found a string of connections that linked their families to a family represented in the show. One woman's college-age daughter was a DeVos girl going to Wayne State. Everyone in Grand Rapids knew a DeVos, or at least knew of them. Another woman had dated a Van Andel. The biggest venue in Grand Rapids was Van Andel Arena. All the stars were real estate developers, were married to real estate developers, or had once been married to a real estate developer, and the names on these developments were familiar, too, plus John was a real estate developer.

The show started with a montage of highlights from the coming season, reminding the audience that all of this had already happened, and there was no way to stop it now.

As the opening credits roll, everyone is introduced with a clip. Rachel, the brunette, leaves a hotel and is picked up by a car. The words "Los Angeles, California" appear beneath the vehicle as it picks up speed on the road. A street sign for Santa Monica Boulevard. A disembodied voice: "I'm on my way to an audition that my husband is holding. He likes me to be there when he and the director are making a final decision about a casting."

"I thought this was about Michigan," Justin whined.

Rachel talks to the camera in a blurry room wearing a different shirt. "I don't expect that everyone has seen my husband's films; I just assume that those who haven't aren't very smart."

The car again: "My husband is a movie producer. A lot of people ask me why we don't live in California, and I tell them, *We'd rather not*. With the way everything is now, no one has to live anywhere anymore to work in Hollywood. He actually produces a lot of movies that are filmed in Michigan, which is great for the economy."

Rachel walks into a carpeted hotel ballroom and shakes the hands of several sitting men. "Hello, hello, hello, so good to see you. Isn't this exciting?" She sits in one of the cushioned metal chairs and kisses the man next to her on the cheek. "Let's get a drink after this, yeah?" She squeezes his bicep. His elbows are on his knees.

"I do think it's my job to be my husband's support system," Rachel says to the camera, answering a question. "He works very hard so we can live the life we do, the way we want to live it. We have a fabulous life here. I wouldn't trade it for anything."

Bella, the redhead, is in an office surrounded by books, telling an assistant where to put one stack of a new delivery. Her testimonial happens in the same office, but in it she is wearing another shirt. "This year, I decided I wanted to get into the family business. I was already on the board, but now I'm CEO of my grandfather's publishing house. Yes, I read." She picks up a book from a stack and holds it up, waving it so the title cannot be made out. "It's my bread and butter. Now my husband, that's another story. He puts food on the table." Her laugh is like a windchime before a storm.

The assistant is holding the stack, walking out the door, when she is called back in. Bella piles a few more books onto the stack and points to something off screen. Her disembodied voice says, "The publishing industry isn't peaking right now, to say the least. But it's what I love to do. Talking to authors, making deals, I love it." She sits in a large leather chair and beckons for another woman to come in, pointing to another large leather chair on the other side of her desk. The two talk and laugh under the voiceover, and then their dialogue gets loud enough to hear.

"Your book is getting rave reviews," says Bella to the woman.

"Rave? I don't know about rave," the woman responds.

"You don't want rave. I shouldn't have said that. It's your first book. Trust me, you want good reviews, not rave. If there's too much attention, people turn on you. There's a guarantee of a backlash for just about every out-the-gate whirlwind success story. You have to temper that flame. Slow and steady, nothing too controversial. Nothing too—nothing overly ambitious."

"I mean, I wouldn't mind a rave review. I don't see that hurting me at this point. One rave review."

"It can hurt you. Trust me. One is the worst number of rave

reviews to have." Bella laughs. "I'm sorry, my assistant should have gotten you a coffee. Tea? Water?"

"I'll have a tea. Do you have green tea?"

"I don't know." She laughs again. They keep speaking while the voiceover returns. "My grandfather started this publishing house as a way to help authors who didn't want to go to New York. You know, New York is New York. He said, *Why not Detroit?* He saw something in the people here. He knew how sensitive they are, how New York wasn't always an option. And some of the best authors are from Michigan. So many artists are moving here now."

Patricia, the blonde, is jogging on a sidewalk flanked with graying mounds of snow. "I'm not really as social as the other girls," says her voiceover as she jogs to her front door and opens it. "I've known Bella and Rachel for years, through our philanthropy. I'm actually closer with Bella's husband than I am with her. I like my privacy, so it was a hard decision to start this new chapter in my life. But I'm an entrepreneur at heart, like my parents were. And my ex-husband. I really learned a lot from that marriage. Yeah. I might have learned even more from the divorce."

Inside the house, her voiceover continues. "Tonight, I'm getting ready for a charity event my company is sponsoring that Bella is coming to as well. I did not invite Rachel, no. To be honest, I've seen her behavior in places with open bars, and I can't have anyone screwing this up for me."

Norma was silent for the entire show, sitting in an armchair close to the screen. At the start of every commercial break, she turned to the rest of us and said, "Well, okay." John grunted every time someone swore, their words muffled by a sustained note. At the top of the hour, he got up from the couch and went outside to the porch.

After the episode, a host interviews only Patricia on a retro sixties stage. They appear to have been watching the show for the first time on a screen behind them. They sit on low-backed swiveling chairs, their heels hooked into bars that loop around the tall metal stands. "You seemed pretty apprehensive about appearing on *Grosse Income*," says the host.

"I was, I was. But you know what? I've made some incredible friendships, as I'm sure you'll see, and overall, I thought it was an opportunity I couldn't pass up."

"Now, opportunity. What do you mean by that?" the host smiles. Her microphone is clipped to her lapel.

"I run a business and I know that promotion is everything. You have to make a good product, but if no one knows about it, it's just as good as a bad product."

"Ah, so the show is a way for your business to get visibility?"

"I say it like I see it. If you don't like it, go tell someone, that's what I say."

"And you really do tell it like it is this season. In fact, the other women don't seem to share the opinion that you are great friends."

"We always have each other's backs. Sometimes we don't like what the other one does, but we all know that nothing will stand between us. We've become extremely close."

"Okay, don't give too much away, now," the host says.

In all my favorite movies, I wrote in my diary, *someone has just died before it starts, or the trouble is covering up a death, or by the end, death is imminent. My mother has died, and so the movie has started. I'm like Cinderella because everyone else has money. I live with my new family who has a second home and a boat on the lake in town, like everyone else in my school. Are princes politicians?*

On the first Monday of our summer break, I got my aunt to pick up Candy from her apartment and bring us to Meijer. I tested Norma, throwing a box of black hair dye into the cart. She looked pained but said sure, as long as we didn't make a mess. We could do it in the bathtub, and it was my bathtub now, anyway, I said to Candy in the backseat of the car, while Norma closed the trunk and walked around to the driver's door.

Once home, we took the potato chips and the dye out of the brown bags on the counter and ran to the basement, tearing each open on the carpeted stairs. Candy reached into her backpack and pulled out two bottles of Robitussin Cough & Cold she'd stolen without me noticing.

First, I showed her the mark on my arm from playing Cherry Bomb. I thought she would be mad at me for hanging out with Lauren, but instead she said, "Baby," and kissed the burn.

"It doesn't hurt anymore," I said.

We made a mess, staining the edges of the sink and rugs with dark purple drops of dye, as thick and toxic as the syrup we drank. The bowl of the sink would definitely be stained near the drain. It didn't matter because no one other than the cleaning lady ever saw this room. There were three other bathrooms in the house. Anyway, I didn't really get in trouble, just humiliated. If they did ever confront me about leaving food in my room or leaving the lights on, I would look away, implying that some things should be taught to girls by their mothers.

Candy ran upstairs and asked one of my cousins for Saran wrap as I sat on the lid of the toilet trying not to move. She ran back downstairs, saying that the boys had looked at her as if she was an alien. "The older one is kind of hot," she said.

"Disgusting," I screamed.

My swirl of hair was dimensionless in the mirror yet it dripped iridescence in the sink. Candy wrapped it in pink plastic film and scrubbed drops from my shoulders, forehead, and ears.

We put towels on the couch and watched TV for twenty-five minutes and then I went back to the bathroom to rinse. I tried with the faucet but found the showerhead easier to manage, so I undressed completely and stepped into the tub. The bottom filled with black that thinned to violet and magenta in beautiful streams and I yelled that it looked crazy. Candy opened the bathroom door. "Let me see it," she said, pulling back the shower curtain. I instinctively backed away.

"What? Let me see it," said Candy, pretending she meant the dye.

The water was hitting Candy in the face. She was squinting and shaking her head, a clown getting sprayed with seltzer. She stripped quickly and got in with me. I'd seen her naked plenty, but never in a shower, her skin lacey with soap. We kissed for what felt like a long time, and then she hopped out, wrapped herself in a towel, and disappeared. The cough syrup started to hit. When I got out, ruining a white towel by wrapping my hair in it, the room was a curtain of falling colors, pink like the syrup and the Saran wrap, purple like the dye when it hit water, yellow like the edges of the stains it left.

Candy was sitting on the couch, standing on the steps, and laying in my bed. I tried to explain that I couldn't tell which one was the real her. The Candy sitting on the couch frowned, offended, which gave me my answer. "Don't worry," I said, stumbling toward her. "I feel great."

Getting high was in and of itself a thing for us to do. We could answer the question, "What do you want to do?" with "Get high," whereas the older kids we knew followed that with another idea.

The first time we got high together, Robert decided to stay sober and trip-sit. Candy presented the bottles like they were two giant rubies by waving a hand along the countertop. "Hold your nose and drink the entire thing at once or else you won't drink enough of it," she said. Cassie had told her what to do but didn't want to be responsible for any of it, and so had left the apartment. She had friends in the building. I watched Candy tip the bottle back and gag. I couldn't do it while holding my nose. The taste was awful, but I downed it, even catching the last drops.

Candy could look like a baby dressed up as an adult and an adult dressed up as a baby. Robert laughed at us rolling around on the floor. He kissed Candy. We watched Lifetime for a while, and then Candy started screaming, like she was pretending to laugh and had forgotten how. Robert muffled her mouth with a cushion, and I took this to mean we were having a pillow fight, but Robert told us we both had to settle down or he was leaving. This made Candy plead with him to stay. He had to go anyway, he said. He'd thought we would be done by then. Candy fell into uncontrollable giggles, not able to catch her breath. "Go ahead," she wheezed, and Robert left, and that was the first time I was ever alone with Candy. I remember sitting very still, just watching her talk, her tiny perfect mouth.

I kept trying to ask the right question, wanting to know if Candy was feeling the same way I was. "It's fun, isn't it?" she would ask in response, and then sink into the couch. We could walk to the Meijer parking lot and ride shopping carts, like we did that one day when we were just stoned, I suggested, but Candy's mom worked at Meijer, and she didn't want to see her just then. We could roll down the hill in the park. The windows had started to bubble, and the carpet was draining of color. We went to the park, the sky darkening like the edges of a Polaroid photo. Everything was doing it, but things would brighten up when I looked straight at them. We sat on the swings in the yard of the closed elementary school. Next came rolling down, but we had to save it because it was going to be the best part.

"We gotta do it now," said Candy. "It's getting dark."

"That's not real," I said, and we laughed until we were on all fours nodding our heads at the ground. "I'm scared," I said, looking up at Candy, and we started laughing all over again, each yelling to the other that she had to stop. "No, of the hill," I said. "I am, though."

"Let's roll down together," Candy said, and grabbed me. We lay flat, kicking each other's legs until they were straight, and then we were like a single rolling pin. When it was over, I sat up and then fell back down, looking at the clouds. It was the most fun I'd ever had in my life. Maybe life was only getting better.

The sky was like a reverse valentine heart, red at the edges with bright white clouds in the middle. We could do that again. It would be cool if it happened just the same way. We did, and it did.

"I'm gonna call my dad to take me home," said Candy.

"You don't want to spend the night?"

"Can't. Your hair looks perfect, though." I didn't ask what she meant by *can't*.

"Did you have fun?" Norma asked as Candy walked out onto the porch toward her father's arriving car. The question sounded pointed. In my room, I listened to music and held a back massager to my crotch. I turned the lights off because the edges of shadows were shaking.

I fell asleep, and when I woke again, it was to the sounds of doors opening and closing, shoes being thrown at a wall to bounce into a basket, and plates being stacked onto a counter in the kitchen above. I assumed it was breakfast, but John called out that it was time for dinner. I didn't know if it was the same day or the next.

I turned on the light and looked into the mirror on my vanity. My hair was not only a new color but a new texture. It was thicker and less shiny. My pupils were still dilated, my mouth pale and small, like a fish's. I tried to relax my face, but my eyebrows kept inching up, dragging the other features with them. I took out a compact and blotted my cheeks. The powder absorbed the color instead of covering it, and then the color returned, a darker flush. I was holding the puff away from my numb skin, maybe. I pressed it hard into the powder so that the cake cracked along its round edge. I wiped and wiped my face with the crumbles. I pinched at my nose, loosening some blackheads. I rolled my skin with my thumb and forefinger. The tiny hairs looked clotted with oil. They looked like strands of pure oil.

Norma yelled that it was dinner time, angrier than John. I passed the powder puff over my face again, and this time it worked. I tried for a neutral expression walking up the stairs.

"Were you napping?" asked Norma, handing me an empty plate, which was lighter than I anticipated, and it bounced up as I took it. "We're having tacos. You can build your own however you like." I tried with everything I had not to laugh, placing limp lettuce and rubbery cheese and beef crumbles on a taco shell.

The conversation at the dinner table always revolved around something that had happened at John's office: a new hire, a tenant late on payment, a setback in construction due to weather. Norma was attempting to include the kids by asking if we wanted to invite friends over for a special dinner. Justin said he couldn't invite only one of his friends, since the other two would find out and get jealous. Dominic looked down at his plate like he was going to cry and said that his best friend would probably like to come over. I had to say something, then. I opened my mouth to speak and already Norma was asking me if I had heard the question.

"Candy," I said, noticing then how funny the name was. I was asking for candy. My cheeks felt fat and hot. *Can candy come. Can-can dancers. Cantaloupe antelope. Candy cane sugar Coca-Cola.*

"The news today was a joke," said John. "They're saying that the Twin Towers couldn't have fallen the way they did just by getting hit by airplanes. I tell you: how do you figure something like that out when nothing like this has ever happened before, in the history of the world?"

"No politics at the dinner table," said Norma.

"Who said anything about politics?" said John.

"I bet you could find that out with a model, though," said Justin. "You could build a replica and fly a miniature plane into it."

"No, because what they're looking at is huge steel beams, and you can't account for the gravity. My real question is: why didn't they come up with this until just now? That's the news for you. What we need to be testing is ways to get terrorists out of the country, not buildings that collapsed last year."

"See, now I think we're getting into politics," said Norma.

The word "terrorists" stumped me on this occasion and others. I was missing something that everyone else understood. There were people called terrorists that were not representative of a certain area, and they did not all ascribe to the same principles, but they were different from other people. They wanted to terrorize. Mothers would call their younger sons "terrors." A puppy could "terrorize" a cat. My taco looked grotesque. If I didn't say something and I wasn't eating, one aberration would draw attention to the other.

"Are terrorists like Jews?" I asked, meaning that similarly, one could be Jewish but not religious, but one didn't have to come from a certain place to be Jewish, either. I had never met a Jew. In school, we learned about the Holocaust and that Jews were displaced from many countries. Around Christmas, we put up Hannukah decorations for an assumed Jewish student. Some kids called each other "Jewy" to mean that they were being cheap. For a long time, I assumed it had something to do with the word "jewelry."

"What? No, not at all," said Norma. "That's a terrible—no."

"Are you—are we Jewish at all?" I asked, noticing I had offended her.

"No, no, we're one hundred percent Dutch," said Norma. "Did your mother not tell you that? Your father is Dutch, too."

Why had she said that? I didn't want my cousins to see me think about my father, who was doing who knows what at this moment, probably playing video games and not thinking about me or his dead ex-wife.

"This is what I'm talking about. You watch the news, and you get everything backwards," said John. The news was terrorizing John. He was so upset with it he sometimes couldn't sleep at night and watched the news instead. He would complain about each segment and its bias. The more he watched, the more he complained, and the more he complained, the more he decided he knew more than what the TV news was reporting, since he was reading the newspaper every day now, too.

It was empowering to know more about what was going on in the world than the rest of the family did, but it was frustrating, too. What were they doing all day, if not reading the news or going to work? Watching reality TV, John said, teaches you what editing does. Anything can be edited to seem more like a story, and real life isn't a story. Well, it is, but it's a pretty unconventional one, with an arc like a heart monitor.

"If we watched real life on TV, and saw news stories that were accurate, we would be bored out of our minds. Everything is for the sake of entertainment. It's just another industry. What about football practice?" he said without changing the tone of his voice, turning to Justin. "Has that started yet?"

There were woods behind the house as far as anyone could see. Deer sometimes drifted into the back yard, which was a cleared hillside. The boys liked to tease me about never having been hunting, fishing, four wheeling, dirt biking, rock climbing, snowmobiling, or skiing. There were many competitive sports that I had never tried. Video games I had never played. Wild animals I had never spotted. I had never killed anything or cleaned dead meat.

Norma and I went on a few quiet walks through the woods right after Sheila died, when everything in the house was too harsh to look at, the dark pounding and the light glinting. She wanted to show me how far back the property went, maybe offering a secluded place for me to be. Justin and Dominic used to have a fort there, where they kept BB guns to shoot birds and squirrels, and where they had played games of paintball with their friends. They listened to their parents because they truly wanted to be like them. They would offer me the last ice cream bar or piece of pie because I was the baby of the family, even if I was the oldest kid.

I woke up to sunlight in my half window. It looked like everyone was gone again. Outside in the declining yard, puffy clouds looked like mice and butts. Spots of color sprouted from them: quilted rays, dotted lines, soap bubbles multiplying under a faucet. I closed my eyes, and they reappeared in the dark, frozen outlines drifting from their centers. A screensaver with a black background getting eaten by neon colors. Swiss cheese holes gasping. I'd heard about people doing one too many tabs of acid and staying that way.

It would be cool, I thought, to be high at work or school, but not at dinner.

I went back inside and called Gina.

"I'm confused," she said. "I thought you hated me."

"Why would you think that?"

"Because you said you did, to Keri."

My body was sliding in two directions. "No, I didn't."

"Yeah, you did. Keri showed me your instant messages."

"But Keri said she hated you first," I whispered.

"Oh my god, you're such a liar."

I hung up and tried to call Keri, but no one picked up.

I went upstairs and checked my emails. Nothing. I wrote to Keri: *You're dead to me.* My last message to the politician was simply, *I would like that,* about us meeting one day, which we'd said would happen many times.

Candy had online pen pals, too. One boy, who she described as "super smart, but with horrible style," went to Columbine High School. She let me read his emails to her. He was seventeen, two years older than her, but she said she was seventeen, too.

He had been a freshman at the time of *the massacre,* he said. Those kids were outsiders, yeah, but they were around. They had some other friends in school. And if it had been a mystery who killed all those people that day, they might not even be suspects. Targeting the guys who played *Doom* and listened to Marilyn Manson would be too obvious. That stuff didn't have any influence over their bloodlust, he argued. If anything, it was the other way around. More likely, they were all surface level interests gained in tandem with, not as precursors to, their nihilistic views and manic depression. But they seemed harmless and even happy sometimes, from what he could remember of them in the hallways between classes. He assumed they had rich lives outside of school because they had such defined senses of style. And they had each other. He, on the other hand, had no close friends in school. It was even more difficult identifying with the murderers once they were murderers, he said.

I went into the master bathroom and pulled the diary out from under the sink and set it on the pink and white bathmat that was puffier in its curlicue roses. The front section of the notebook took on more volume than the second half, showing me that Sheila hadn't used most of it, even after five years. Each entry could be marking the most special of occasions, like Christmas cards updating the rest of the family, time capsules meant to see the past from a future perspective, notes to a daughter once she was an adult. I had taken the cordless phone with me into the bathroom. Its small siren startled me. I braced myself, thinking it would be Gina or Keri.

"I lost my virginity," said Candy. For a moment I thought she was referring to what we had done in the shower. Then she said that Robert had come over once she got home, and that they had had sex on her bed. Sex with Robert was perfect, exactly what she'd imagined, and not worth waiting for only because there was no real reason to wait. She wished that she'd been having sex the whole time, which was almost a school year. In retrospect I had assumed, without really thinking about it, that Candy's romantic and intellectual relationship with Robert was above sex.

I don't regret it, Sheila scribbled, in 1997. *Maybe I do. But I would have left him even if I hadn't met someone else. I know that. Maybe it would have taken longer. I have to be grateful to Curtis for that, even if I hate him now.*

I didn't know a Curtis. I tried to scan the notebook for any other mention of his name and found none.

He was probably cheating on me. Seems like they all do.

I didn't know to which he this *He* referred. *Seems like they all do* could mean both Curtis and my father, and anyone else.

I took off my apron and went outside, pretending to need a cigarette. Some of the RNs had smoke breaks in their cars with the radios on. If there was no one standing by the door smoking, I just sat in the sun, watching my skin redden and the parked cars spit exhaust. The burn on my arm still ached when I was near the dishwasher or the hot top. It bulged, its edges papery in the strong daylight. No one was watching me take my break and so I went back inside to clock out. The air conditioning vacuumed me through the door and down the hall, where I could hear Genie whimpering. I followed the sound of her voice, toward the residents' rooms, entering the North wing for the first time.

Genie sat near an open door at the intersection of the wings. Beyond us was a room I had never noticed before, one with more chairs and another TV, but no tables. A commercial for a vitamin subscription service played soundlessly. Genie wasn't making any moves to enter. A soap opera's theme song drifted from somewhere else. Either the music or the smell of this wing made my stomach twist. Genie's face looked breakable.

"Hello," I said as casually as possible, stopping in front of the wheelchair.

Genie gave a high-pitched mumble and dug her hands into the pockets of her powder blue cardigan.

"How are you?"

"Meh, mmm," said Genie. "No, no, no. Oh, no."

"Is something wrong?"

"Oh, yes. Oh. Oh. My sister. Lovely, lovely."

"Is your sister visiting?" I asked.

"She's here. She's—oh, God—she's my sister, she's." Genie's sister never visited, from what I knew. She was probably dead. Genie talked about her more than she talked about her dead husband, though.

"I'd like to meet her. Is she younger?"

"No! No. I just saw her, she's."

An RN passing by us looked at my open face and at Genie's worried hands. He didn't slow down but said, "Calm down Genie, it's all gonna be okay." I relaxed my eyebrows. Genie acknowledged the nurse's absence by reaching toward my apron's doubled waist ties and curling her fingers around them. I'd been told by one of the RNs not to touch the residents, for my own safety. "You don't know what they get into."

Still, I shook Genie's hand loose and held it. As I knelt to the ground, tears streamed down her face, quietly and without warning. I felt the backs of my eyes getting hot. My surroundings came into focus. It wasn't like I was visiting a relative or even volunteering, in fact I wasn't even working anymore, I was off the clock, but I wasn't getting up to leave, either. Genie and I were holding hands in a fluorescently lit hallway, eyes in our laps, minds getting closer to the same pace. We each said nothing for what seemed like a long time.

I had never seen a resident cry with tears before, though I sometimes heard them sniffling or bellowing and I saw them rubbing their eyes with their knuckles. Of all of them, I wouldn't have guessed Genie, the class clown, to be weepy. Perhaps it was me. I had coaxed a cat out from under the bed after everyone else had tried. I could say anything I wanted to, then. I told Genie, in a whisper, that I wished none of them had to live there and be pushed around by younger, stronger people. I started to move away, but Genie's eyes met mine then and I felt my hand being held tighter, surprised by how strong her grasp felt under crêpe skin. She opened her mouth and said a lot of sounds starting with B. Another RN I had never met walked up to us and stopped. I turned my crouching body and saw that she was staring at the soles of my cheap shoes.

"Is she bothering you?" the RN asked. I wasn't sure who she was talking to. "Come on now, let's just relax, 'kay?"

"Come on. Kay?" mimicked Genie, who let go of my hand and then was being wheeled backwards, away, and forward, down the hall to her room.

My mother always had a new tube hanging out of her when I visited the hospital, a massive building downtown I would have walked right past had I no reason to be there. I was vaguely aware of tests and drips and biopsies, all trying to figure out where the cancer had started, rather than how to stop it. There was no stopping it, the doctors knew when they met her. She would see me look down at her bruised arms and say, "Don't look at all that. You don't want to know," and she was right.

She was on painkillers, but they didn't always work. I could tell because she would try to shift in her bed and an involuntary sound would escape her crinkled mouth, which embarrassed her in front of me. She pulled the covers up to her chest to hide how much of her body had disappeared. Her speech was slow, either from pain or from the killing of it. Her skin, which was thinner, and the whites of her eyes, which were thicker, yellowed. Still, she would pull her lips into a smile when she saw me, and I would try to pretend I was just visiting my mother in bed, in her room at home. I would tell her about my day and ask who sent flowers.

"I'm not so into those," she'd say, and we would both hear the old her, so we would sustain the moment.

"Why would anyone think you like those?" I would say, having to measure my enthusiasm. Too much would make her tired, and too little would make her frustrated. Eventually, she was not able to eat or breathe without machinery, and she had drugs pumping non-stop through her system. She was moved, somehow, to hospice, and

I was encouraged to stay away until she was ready. Ready to die, I later understood. When I die, I thought, I do not want anyone around to see it.

After, when I'd go downtown and walk near the hospital, I'd see all of it: first the gaping entrance and then the rest, so tall and wide I couldn't take it in statically. Now, it was something else, not a boring building to look past and not a place to visit after school. The traffic through the sliding doors was so heavy, they never fully closed, and I felt a conveyer-smooth pull toward the horrible fluorescence inside. I watched skateboarders do tricks in front on railings. Their legs had no knees in their big Gumby pants. There was no outline of a bone to break. The sound of the wheels going over sidewalk seams was a ball scuttling over a roulette wheel but endless.

The doorbell sounded upstairs, and Norma yelled down to me. Everyone else always came in through the garage, so it had to be Candy. I had changed out of my work shirt into a polyester tank top but left my work pants on. We sat in the upstairs TV room and watched the news with John while my cousins took their own friends into their separate rooms. We could all hear Norma sighing.

"Do you want help with dinner?" Candy called into the kitchen.

"Oh no, don't worry about it." Something stopped me from inviting Candy to my room, to be alone with her there. We heard "Dinner's ready" and got up from the sofa while John searched for the remote without moving his eyes from the screen. The sound of socked feet on carpeted steps and dirty palms squeaking down bannisters made Norma smile. Two store-bought precooked chickens sat in the center of the table. On each of our plates were mashed potatoes and buttered peas. Candy sat down first and stared at her plate, then looked at me with her whole head. I didn't look back.

"Tess," she whispered.

"What."

"Rotisserie."

I knew she would make fun of my family somehow, and right in front of them. Her father never made dinner. She usually made herself spaghetti from a box or salad from a bag or something from the freezer, while Cassie went to her friends' apartments or ordered pizza, but Candy was quick to judge everyone with money for not using it correctly. "Trash," she'd say about the classmates' houses she'd seen over the years, back when she was invited to classmates' birthday parties. Tanning beds that took up the whole basement, tennis courts that no one used anymore, paintings of pets that only the mother missed. "What a waste."

While John was saying grace, Candy yanked at my hand. I didn't have to bow my head and close my eyes because everyone else was doing it, so they wouldn't notice me not doing it. Everyone took a deep breath after "amen."

"So, Candy. What do you think of *Grosse Income*?" Norma asked. She laughed at herself. "I think it's kind of fun."

"I love it," said Candy. "It's so stupid."

"Oh, I mean, I wouldn't mind being on it." Norma suddenly looked toward the kitchen, maybe having forgotten something in the oven.

"On it?" asked Dominic. "What do you mean?"

"I mean, not moving there, just, being on a, being part of a documentary."

"That's generous," said John. "Extremely generous."

"I was kind of joking," said Norma.

"Why not?" asked Candy. "Being famous is better than being rich, and being rich and famous is better than being just one or the other."

"No," I said. "You're not serious."

"Yes, I am," said Candy.

"Well, I know someone on the show," I said.

"Everyone does," said Justin.

"And you didn't say anything while we were watching it?" asked Norma.

"I wasn't sure it was him until," I looked up at her. She was biting her lip. Both of her hands were on the table.

"Well? Who is he? How do you know him?"

"Yeah, Tess," Candy laughed. "How do you know him?"

"Just someone I know from Ypsi," I said. "Not well. He was just, around."

Norma's shoulders relaxed. "Point him out next time," she said, quietly. John had finished a plate and was going in for seconds. Justin and his friend started to tell a story about a football game or practice or something, and then Candy said, "Wow, sports," stunning them both into silence.

"I want to get into a good college," said Justin's friend. "So, yeah, sports."

"What college?" asked Candy. She had a big book at home, like a phone book, with every college in the country and its up-to-date statistics: tuition, class size, ranks.

"Michigan State," said Justin's friend.

"Tess," said John, his eyes suddenly bright. "You're going to apply there, right?" John had gone to Michigan State.

"Probably not," I said.

"Why not?"

"Because I don't want to go there. Or anywhere."

"Oh, come on," said John.

"John," said Norma.

"If I don't go to college, what happens?" I could hear my voice starting to break, and so I made it louder. "If I don't get a scholarship, I can't go anyway." I folded peas into potatoes.

"We've gone over this, Tess," said Norma, gently.

"Listen," interrupted John. "We made an agreement, as far as I'm concerned." John was almost a lawyer when he was younger. "Taking care of a person your age means making sure they go to college. End of story. Everyone goes to college these days. If you don't like it, tough."

All four of the boys, their cheeks flushed and their smiles fading, swallowed each bite. They seemed shorter now, in their chairs.

"I don't like it," I said. I dropped my fork onto my plate and got up. Once I was standing, I had to go somewhere, so I left the dining room and went down the hall. I stopped. "And I told you," I said, not quite loud enough, "Candy is a vegetarian." I ran down the basement stairs, to my room. Candy got up and followed behind me. I could hear John telling me to get back there and Norma telling him to let me go and the boys and their friends saying nothing.

Candy held me and told me not to cry, even though I wasn't crying. We were in my bed. "Want to see the sex positions I did with Robert?" she asked. "I can show you."

She hovered over me, touching my chest with both hands from behind. Next, she was on her back, pulling my body over hers. She asked if I was getting horny.

"No," I said, pulling back.

"I am," Candy said, and she kissed me. Then she kissed each of my cheeks as if they had tears on them, saying, "You know I love you." She had said this before, but it meant something else now. For Candy, maybe it had always had this meaning. She had a boyfriend because of course she did, and I would too, one day, but we belonged to each other in another way. Her dad was going to pick her up soon. She told me to come back to her apartment with her when he did. I went upstairs and told Norma I was spending the night at Candy's. She seemed hurt, but she let me go, telling me, like always, to call her when I got there, even though I never did. We waited on the front porch.

"Let's go to Meijer," said Candy, in the car. "Mom's not working."

Her dad was a cheerful man who never pried. "I was a teen once," was one of his favorite things to say. "You don't gotta tell me twice," was another. He was inured to his daughters' screaming fights and slamming doors, even when the doors were slammed on him. He thought Robert was a "great guy," even though Robert couldn't make eye contact with anyone. He even had only nice things to say about Candy's mother, who was supposedly an angry drunk who screened his calls.

At the store, I went straight to the barrels and put some gummies into a cellophane bag using a metal scoop. Candy didn't like candy, but she squealed at the sight of ripe, fresh fruit. Meijer had the biggest produce department of any store in the city. Every aisle was a silver point on a pinwheel as we pushed each other on a shopping cart, stopping short so one of us would double over and almost flip into the basket. Candy's dad took the cart away, as a joke, saying we were "too wacked out to drive," and so we went to the play area and mounted a thickly enameled metal horse and duck. After pulling at the animals stiffly, we noticed that they were not on springs but posts, with gears. They cost a quarter each. A man bagging groceries stared at us.

"Got a quarter?" yelled Candy.

"It means you're gonna ride that thing?" he said. The customer he was helping thanked him and pushed her cart away.

"What do you think?" I asked.

Candy got off the horse and pulled me from the duck. "That was gross," she said.

"We should have just done it," I said. "To see what else he would say."

"That's why I love you," she said. "You're secretly perverted."

"I do want to go to college," I said.

"It's okay if you don't," said Candy.

"I mean, I want to get out of here."

"As far away as humanly possible."

"Where?" I asked.

"Fucking anywhere. Look at this place." We caught the eye

of the grocery bagger again, and he smiled, then cocked his chin at us.

"Girls, let's go," said Candy's dad, a paper bag resting on each forearm.

I can't tell you everything I know about Candy's family, the stuff she told me later. I know you don't know her anyway, but it doesn't feel right. Her dad was not as great of a guy as I'd thought, and her mom went through a lot. But this was all told to me when Candy was less lucid, during one of her diatribes that felt more like a net to keep me listening than a cathartic conversation.

Sometimes it's a relief to not be close to anyone I'm related to. I know that sounds harsh. I wouldn't say I'm estranged from anyone, just, no one became my replacement mom, and my dad was never that into holidays, and it's easy to get away with doing whatever I want because everyone assumes I'm with someone else, like friends. It's lonely on birthdays if I don't plan anything, but I don't know, you probably talk to your parents once a week, if not more, and that seems like time that might be better spent.

No, think about it. You ask them about a lease agreement or a tax form or something and they want to ask how you're doing otherwise, and then you sit there and remember your entire childhood, how someone cheated on someone or walked in on you doing something obscene or admitted they had a favorite child and then told you exactly why, with a hand, that kind of thing. I'm lucky, because none of that stuff ever needs to come up for me. I never have to think about any of it again.

We stayed up late watching movies under one blanket in the living room and fell asleep there, on the floor. In the morning, Robert picked us up to go to Blues on the Mall. The highway was the only route to anywhere from where we lived, anywhere other than Walgreen's, the smaller grocery stores, bike repair shops, florists, Blimpie, or a cafeteria with a marquee that advertised an early bird special starting at six. These places looked sad and run down, nothing to unblur one's eyes for until Candy pointed at them, saying something about each site like a tour guide for teenagers. "That gas station doesn't card for cigarettes, that's that girl Riley's house, and she pretends she doesn't have money." I sighed loudly when we passed Berrylawn, and she knew exactly what I meant, that work sucks, but, she added, "You like having a job, or else you wouldn't have one."

"I need a job," I said.

"You did need a job," she corrected, "before you moved in with your rich aunt and uncle. Now, you don't want to quit."

It was true that time felt different there, that I was a different person when I was in my uniform and only interacting with people twice or six times my age.

"There it is," Candy said, moving on, as we passed one of the other Berrylawn buildings. "Where Cassie went."

Candy's sister and three of her friends, all seniors, had been admitted to Berrylawn Psychiatric at one point. They had stories about the awful food and the annoying counselors who made you talk about your drug use in a large group. Berrylawn was the name of the entire complex, so Sheila had technically been to Berrylawn, too, meaning the hospice. It was strange to hear the name mean something other than a place to work or die. Every teen who said they'd been to Berrylawn meant Psychiatric, though, usually because they were caught with weed or very drunk.

In books, getting checked into a psych ward meant staying there for years, fighting demons off and finding all new ones in the people you'd be stuck with there. Cassie and her friends went for a few days each, as a warning against wearing black lipstick and listening to bands with names that frightened parents, like Christian Death. It was sparsely decorated, even for a medical facility, except for all the plastic leather Bibles, Cassie told us. Half a week there was a good scare tactic, letting bratty girls suffer the indignities of cold lighting, one-channel TVs, mandatory sleep aids, and waxy-sheeted beds, but it was also a place to meet likeminded kids. Cassie had gone after an intense argument with her mother that ended with each of them running around a parking lot, shoeless. They couldn't remember how the fight had started, but the point of no return was when Cassie stepped on glass and then held the bloodied piece up like a weapon.

After blocks and blocks of Berrylawn came a graveyard that rose and fell along the road, then thinned to a horizon line as we merged. I never quite saw it end, since no one ever drove me further in that direction before taking the next turn. The downtown exit gave the illusion that Grand Rapids was a big city because from an elevated road the buildings crowded together and launched from behind one another, sparkling skyscrapers and historic monuments. From there, though, we took a dirt-lined hill to a swinging traffic light and a regular left turn to the dilapidated neighborhood where only ethnic minority families lived.

Our entire high school was white. The Bosnian and Croatian refugees were there because our district was deemed a haven for immigrants, even if at school they were all ridiculed. I'd walked into a classroom in which the message "Bosnians go home" was written on the whiteboard, not knowing yet which ones were the refugees. A girl who I had assumed was Russian from her sexy accent and dated clothes had walked in behind me, but upon seeing the words, she turned around and went back down the hall, through the front double doors, out to the lawn. I couldn't tell if she was offended or if she had taken the words literally.

Entering downtown, we saw the skyscrapers again, this time looking spaced out and not as tall. Banks, bars, galleries, and the hospital each had a Dutch name. Some restaurants were Dutch-themed, their bathrooms decorated with fake tulips and windmill paintings, but served American diner food; none of us knew what Dutch food was. Robert became exasperated trying to find a parking spot and settled for a ten-dollar lot if we agreed to help pay for it.

I looked at my reflection in windows as we walked toward the festival. Some patches of my hair were not quite black, and I tried to tuck them underneath the rest. I had to balance the harshness of the new color with even more eyeliner. Candy said I looked beautiful and held my hand. The crowd was bigger than I'd expected and more diverse in age. The lot of Harley Davidson motorcycles mostly had old men on them. People dancing to the fuzzy echoes made by an old blues band were old, too. And there were parents with kids eating ice cream, even babies in strollers holding balloon animals.

It was a regular street fair, something like the ones my friends and I had grown out of in Ypsi. "I don't get it," I said, daring Candy or Robert to defend this scene. They had huge smiles on their faces. Together they ran to a cart selling funnel cake and I had the choice of running after them or getting lost. We wove around the stage, searching for people we recognized.

"Quit dragging up the rear," laughed Robert, glancing behind him.

Candy led. "It was so much better when there were grassy knolls," she said, pausing at a higher vantage point.

"What's a grassy knoll?" I asked.

I couldn't believe they would rather be in the thick of this generic moment instead of listening to music they liked at home. I sat on some cement steps, complaining that I was too tired to keep aimlessly walking. And then I saw Stephen and his two friends. They were smoking cigarettes and slithering out of the crowd. They hated it here, too, I could tell. But there they were. Maybe Candy was right about the grassy knolls. I pulled her wrist. "That's him," I said.

She asked Robert if he knew who he was.

"Which one?"

"The guy with the tight pants over there."

"Oh, Stephen? Yeah, he's a piece of shit."

"Tess has a crush on him."

"Stop," I said.

"On Stephen? Don't. He's a piece of shit."

"What do you mean?" asked Candy.

"He's a piece of shit is what I mean."

Stephen slipped out of view behind a building, so I waited to see him on the other side. Staring at the little gap between one building and the next, the sidewalk and the building started to meld, and I thought I might have been staring at the thing instead of the absence of it and that was how I had missed him. He was gone, and so were his friends, into a maze of reflective windows. A guy wearing wire-framed glasses and a black trench coat came up the steps to talk to Robert.

"You should like *him*," Candy whispered.

I tried to pay attention, but the image of Stephen glimmered back, a mirage on the desert of ugly people, people I'd never seen before and would never otherwise notice. I looked up, trying to be casual, but the guy in the glasses was already walking away. Robert handed us each a tiny plastic bag decorated with a blue design of repeating Batman symbols. "Don't take it yet," warned Robert. We stuffed the pills into our pockets.

When Sheila and I still lived with him, my father worked in other towns a lot, as a foreman or just, as he'd say, a worker. Right after he and Sheila divorced, I saw him more often, or at least more intensely than when they were married, since I would go visit him at my grandmother's house in Dexter. She died, too, and I remember the funeral, my dad moving out of Michigan, my mom moving us to Grand Rapids, and then the diagnosis, but I can't remember the order of any of it. I could ask Norma about it if I wanted to, to put it all back into focus, but I haven't.

On those visits to Dexter, I probably didn't talk to my dad about much, but the things we did discuss would bob up as memories later, topics floating in time instead of discussions at Grandma's lace table-cloth surrounded by glass-doored displays of Delftware. I'd wanted to go to college, then, and he explained what that would mean. I needed better grades than the average student, since it was a competition that involved factors like money and sway, which we didn't have. I couldn't count on having some story to get me a scholarship, like being a refugee or orphan, he said. I would miss my friends if I moved away, he said. He missed his friends. Sheila had said that anyone could be replaced, that making new friends was underrated.

Once, not so long ago, my dad told me as if it was nothing, that he hadn't decided he wanted a kid, that it was all Sheila's idea. He said, "She would've had a kid with someone else if it wasn't me," and then laughed.

Cassie had acquired a pint of Popov for us, and Candy had poured it into a water bottle so we could take turns drinking it on the street. Robert never drank because he used to, and when he did, he hated himself even more, Candy said. The two of them talked into one another's ears, back and forth, walking in front of me. Then Candy stopped and turned around to face me. I reached for the bottle.

"I think I have to go home," she said.

"Why?"

"I have to go home," she repeated.

"Did you take that pill already?" Robert asked.

"No, I promise."

"You're freaking out because of your meds mixing with alcohol, then."

"I have to go *home*," said Candy again.

"Fine," Robert said. "Does she need a ride?" He nodded sideways at me. I didn't answer, since I wasn't being asked.

Candy didn't say anything, either. She looked at the pavement, marked up with a chalk drawing of Earth or a face. "Robert. Robert?"

"What?"

"Please take me home?"

"I said okay," he said.

It was still light out. Sometimes Candy would have these outbursts, but I knew she would relax when I could be alone with her and stroke her head like a cat's. I repeated my own name in my head, not hearing it from either of them. Lauren was walking by herself near the bandshell. "I don't need a fucking ride," I said.

Other summers bleed into this one, the one during which I lost my virginity and saw another death up close. I have some clues that place certain events onto other years, other places. Other times I was doing drugs and kissing people and jumping up and down at shows and throwing glass bottles at walls happened in other summers or weekends while school was in session, or even late weeknights, when I would sneak out of the house, maybe hoping to be caught.

Whenever I've gone back to Grand Rapids, the same men were around, not growing up in the way I was because they were already older. I've gone home with some but no longer let time collapse like that. I try not to return to anyone, mostly because I'm old enough that these men don't seem so much older than me.

This summer must have been pivotal. What about the way things turned out has turned me into what I am—and what, exactly, am I? Single, again, each relationship more serious than the last. Do I have a type? My friends think so. You think so. But I can see that all these people are different from one another. They only look and act the same.

When I picture my mother now, I don't think about a sick person in a bed, not at first. I think about her driving, exasperated by traffic, with me in the passenger seat, pausing what I'm telling her about something that happened at school, suddenly aware of the anecdote's triviality. "Just a *minute*," she says, talking to the wider world, but directing the plea to me, a component she can somewhat control.

She pushes the button that turns off the radio, letting her hand jump back on the spring of her wrist. I know people who have died of other ailments, mostly self-induced. Sometimes I have the horrible thought that if she hadn't gotten cancer, she would have gotten something else, not because our fates are lined up like bowling pins that will topple one way or another, but because some people don't seem to understand how to hold onto life. I picture a steering wheel spinning away from her hands right after she silences me and the song that was playing, the trees reaching over us.

I wonder what her life would be like now, with an adult daughter like me, but increasingly, that scenario feels inconsequential, a pointless hypothetical. The truth is we would consume different types of content, try or not to see eye to eye about that and about, you know, issues, art, politics, anything. We would argue, I guess, over things about which I would later stop caring. We would connect over a TV show and have discussions about its characters that would stand in for how we felt toward one another. We would leave a lot more things unsaid than what we've left unsaid as it is.

"I'm mad at Candy," I told Lauren. "And I have this pill." I handed her the bag. "Do you have one of those indexes?"

One thing about Lauren was that she would stop whatever she was doing if something seemed more interesting.

We walked to a parking structure and got into her car. She drove us to Walgreen's. We searched the greeting card section and magazine rack before finally finding the drug book in the checkout line. It said that the pill, which had a tiny hole in the shape of a K, was clonazepam.

"People make meth out of that, I think," said Lauren. "You ever done heroin?"

"No," I said, maybe too quickly. Obviously, I hadn't.

"I have."

She was probably lying. "How was it?"

"Pretty rad," Lauren started laughing because we were at the head of the line, and I had not put the book back. "I snorted it, but I don't mind needles. I get a shot in my ass every month for birth control. It was just that no one had any." Lauren took the book out of my hands and had the cashier scan it. She paid for it and a pack of Marlboros with her cousin's expired ID.

There were things that were unquestionably bad, like death and senselessly inflicting pain on others. Self-harm was not unquestionably bad. Drugs were not bad either. In fact, they were the best. But heroin was worse for some reason. Dangerous was a better word than bad. But all drugs were dangerous. And so many things that I used to think of as good were in fact bad and vice versa. Organized religion was bad. But where did organization start, and where did religion end?

I asked Lauren for a cigarette to smoke in her car. If she'd done heroin, how bad could it be? She wanted to go to the coffee shop. She didn't want a coffee; she just wanted to go there. She would go out of her way to be around, even if it was obvious no one explicitly wanted her there. I wished I could be like that. We parked in the lot and got out of the car. I scanned the room for Stephen through the window before we went inside. He wasn't there. I ordered a coffee.

"Why does Candy hate me?" Lauren asked, when we were sitting at a table.

"I don't think she does." I was bad at lying. Lauren looked away because she recognized this.

Lauren came from a rich family. Ever since they were little, said Candy, she always got everything she wanted at Christmas and would bring her toys to school to show everyone. People stopped liking her because she couldn't stop showing off. And that's when Lauren became interested in alternative things. She understood her classmates' measured indifference toward her as bullying and started to act out. Since she had often been the only person to raise her hand in class, her first form of protest was presenting ignorance. No more getting every answer right, or even paying attention. Some kids found this annoying, too, since it made for one less buffer. "Lauren? Want to take a stab at it?" their geometry teacher would say, all but winking. "I didn't hear the question," she'd reply, all but putting a leg up on the desk.

I could never get away with this behavior as a new kid because no one knew if I was smart or not. Candy was always raising her hand with the answer, but she was somehow always getting sent to the counselor. She was either a teacher's favorite, because she asked the most questions, or least favorite, for the same reason. Everyone knew about her tantrums from childhood, and so they would test her. "Stop," Candy would say, a little too loudly, "kicking . . . my . . . chair."

"Excuse me?" our biology teacher would ask, still facing the blackboard.

"Nothing," and four seconds later, "I said, stop," in the voice of someone chased by deadly bees. The whole room would laugh, and she'd yell, "Fuck you, I wasn't talking to you" to another guy and be given detention. She had the reputation of a girl possessed, someone who was weird even as a little kid.

Hours went by and no one I recognized came into the coffee shop, but Lauren, as if stuck there, as if passing the time because she had to, told me stories about the regulars. One guy was in jail for breaking and entering some girl's bedroom at night and stealing her underwear. Now that he was out, though, the girl was secretly dating him. Her parents couldn't know because they were the ones who pressed charges. Another guy was an art teacher at one of the Christian colleges and married his student, then got fired. There was a patron of the arts, mainly poetry, who would have fondue parties at his house. He and his wife had a bathtub in their living room and a giant gong they would sound when it was the time of the evening when people had to undress. Lauren had never been, but she'd heard.

Two girls with straightened black hair wearing black clothing walked in. Looking at them, I felt like a stack of tires. "Rose, Fallon," Lauren said, smiling from her seat. The girls turned their heads. They seemed disappointed to see Lauren, or simply disappointed, but walked over anyway and introduced themselves: Rose and Fallon. I asked if they were related. They were not sisters, no, although they got that all the time. Lauren asked what was going on that night.

"There's a party at Stephen's I guess, but this one doesn't want to go." Fallon pointed a thumb at Rose.

"Stephen? Which?" I said, even though I didn't know Stephen's last name, or how he spelled it, or where he lived.

"My ex," said Rose.

"I wanna go," said Lauren. Obviously, Stephen had dated someone like Rose, and obviously if she didn't want to go to his party now, it was because he had dumped her or cheated on her or did something else to hurt her. I was so stupid, to have had a crush on him without even thinking that there were girls like this that lived here.

A man who looked Hispanic or Middle Eastern or Italian opened the door. He wore a soft pack of cigarettes folded into his t-shirt sleeve, which I had only ever read about happening in books. His arms were big but not so big that the pack lay flat. He had a funny walk, sort of a limp, and he touched his head and raised his eyebrows when he ordered coffee, unrolling the sleeve and shimmying a single cigarette up, pulling it out with his mouth. "Rose," he said, nodding, and then, "Fallon."

"Are *you* going to Stephen's?" Fallon asked.

"Maybe swing by there. Got band practice with him anyway, unless it's cancelled."

"Need a ride?" Lauren said.

"Could need that." He blinked slowly.

"What's your name?" Lauren asked.

"I'm Mickey," he said, lighting the cigarette, confidently drunk, I thought.

"Should we pre-game?" asked Lauren. "Who wants to buy us booze?" She pointed at the door. "That store doesn't take my ID."

Mickey took some money from Lauren and told us to wait there while he went across the street. He came back with a pint of Black Velvet and another pack of Basic reds, which I didn't point out to Lauren when he handed her the change. "You girls wanna come to my spot?" His eyes were greenish brown. "We can walk from here."

Fallon and Rose stayed behind, Fallon saying she would talk Rose into going to the party. "I hate parties," sulked Rose. I couldn't imagine.

A few blocks away, we all sat on a porch and passed the bottle around.

I asked to use Lauren's cell phone and walked to the sidewalk, then called home to tell Norma I was spending the night.

"Not two nights in a row," said Norma.

"But that was Candy. This is Lauren."

"We haven't met Lauren, have we?"

"I don't know. She's picked me up from your house before."

"Not tonight. I can come get you now or after dinner, your choice."

"I'm having dinner with Lauren's family. They live really far away. I just forgot to tell you until now. It's not a big deal. Her parents want me to stay."

I pictured this, Lauren's old, rich parents, sitting on their armchairs while a fire roared underneath a mounted head. It was impossible to believe. Parents of teenagers don't really want anyone coming over.

"I can pick you up, it's no problem. I can leave right now."

"No, no, I'll get a ride."

I walked slowly back to the porch, where everyone was more relaxed than before, and told Lauren she could drop me off before going to the party. I knew she'd do it, but I didn't know she'd pretend to get mad at me first. "Fuck, I just started drinking," she said. I said she could take her time, and she did, waiting for the whole pint to be gone and then smoking another cigarette. "You gonna be here after I drop her off?" she said.

"I'll go with," said Mickey. "I love a car ride." I blushed, imagining what Mickey would think of my half-mile long driveway lined with the neighbors' show horses. "Shotgun," he added.

I got into the back seat. Mickey liked Lauren, or else he wouldn't have asked to ride with us, with her, up front. She laughed and sped on the highway, saying, "Is this scary?" because she was drunk. We were slowing toward my aunt and uncle's address when Mickey twisted around and looked at me.

"Hey little girl," he said. He reached out and put a knuckle under my chin. "I'll see you again, right?"

Lauren glanced at the rearview.

"Okay," I squeaked. He nodded, then turned back to the windshield, maybe looking at the big house where I lived. Everyone was silent. "Here's fine," I said, and got out of the car. It sped off and I walked to the house as a neon sun set.

I slumped past the whole family watching TV, saying nothing, even after Norma barked, "Hel-lo?"

Everyone is at the party, and I am missing it, I wrote in my diary, then underlined every word for emphasis.

"Your father called," John shouted down the stairs.

The word *father* was a serrated blade. I used the phone in the kitchen to call him back after I finished watching a rerun on the basement TV.

"How's it goin' up there?" he asked, his voice so close, not echoing down a tunnel or fuzzing over a radio like I'd imagined. I had still never been to where he lived, or anywhere out of state. I tried to remember if it was Ohio or Iowa. He'd moved around for one job, and then another job, and then he lost that job, I was pretty sure, but ended up staying there, wherever it was.

"Good," I said.

"Oh, is it?" he asked. I must have sounded genuine. "That's good to hear. Guess that means you wanna stay, right?"

"What do you mean?"

"Oh, I don't know." We both stopped thinking about the question.

"How's it going . . . down there?" I asked.

"Oh, it's going. Trying to get this work thing to work, you know. I'll get it one day. Hey, but listen, I'm supposed to head up to Ypsi at the end of the summer and was thinking I could come scoop you up on the way, if it doesn't interfere with your schooling and whatnot."

Only days before, the idea of visiting my old friends would have woken me from a stupor. I thought back to the last phone conversations I'd had with them. Even before I knew that Gina hated me for hating her, it felt as though everything had moved ahead for all of them, and since Mickey touched my face just minutes ago, things seemed to be moving ahead for me, too. I put my hand in my pocket and held the little plastic baggie.

"Okay," I said, because I didn't know what else to say to my father.

"Oh, it's good to hear that voice," he said. "John and Norma treating you nice? They got all them horses and space and everything, it's gotta be pretty nice, right?"

"The horses don't belong to them," I said. "I've never even ridden one." I was suddenly drunker, almost forgetting who it was I was talking to. I sounded like someone else. Words kept leaving my mouth. "If I had a horse," I trailed off. "I don't know their names. Maybe I should ask them."

My dad laughed, like I'd made a joke. "Hey sweetheart," he said, and I felt sick, feverish. "I gotta head out."

"Yeah," I said, in awkward agreement.

I hung up the phone, then went upstairs to the computer. The politician's messages were about his life, mostly. How much he traveled, how I should travel, too. There's a wide world out there, especially for someone like me, he'd say. I didn't know what that meant. I told him I had no money, and he insisted that money wasn't what was keeping me anywhere. In a way, he was right. The thing that was keeping me here was my age. Once I was an adult, though, it would be money.

When we messaged, he said he wanted to make sure I knew how special I was, that this was something about which he felt strongly. I said I wasn't sure. I said it was so cool that he was on *Grosse Income*. He explained that it was just for publicity, that he wasn't very close with any of those people. As a politician, you must get your name out there, he said. I was sure they hadn't mentioned his name.

"None of that stuff is real, you know," he wrote. "It's smoke and mirrors. The party didn't even have music playing, because then they wouldn't be able to edit the sound right later."

"It wasn't a real party?"

"It was and it wasn't. What is a party, anyway?"

"A party has music," I wrote.

"Indeed."

"So, it was all fake?"

"No. It was all real. A real party that was thrown for a TV show."

"I wish I could go to a party like that."

"Maybe next time," he wrote.

"But your wife," I typed, then deleted. He hated when I brought that up. Instead, I said, "I hope so."

"You're an incredible person, I can tell," he wrote.

"Thank you," I said, and meant it.

"You'll do something very great one day," he wrote.

"And what if I don't?" I replied, after thinking about it.

"You will still be incredible to me," he said.

He said he had to go, so I signed off and shut down the computer. I went into the master bathroom and locked myself in, retrieved the diary, and read from it on the floor.

Sometimes I wish I could start over with people, like my ex (ex!) husband. Not that I did anything so bad. People can only hear so much before they can't stand . . . Everything piles onto all the other things you've ever said, and you can't take any of that back. I would sometimes just talk for the sake of it, so that everything I said before would be replaced and forgotten. You can never start over, though. You can't just start talking in a new way and say this is the new me.

Norma and John were not bad people. They worried about their children, about spoiling them, about how they might hurt themselves. Each of the boys had broken something somehow, snowboarding or sledding or getting dragged on a tube from the back of a car. None of the boys were bad either.

The dinner, it turned out, was meant to announce that the family was moving to a bigger house, one with a room for me that wasn't in the basement. I'd be going to college soon anyway, but I'd need a place to come back to in the summer. The summers.

My room was perfect, with lots of light, on the top floor, said Norma, with tears in her eyes. Like light was what would make me happy. I imagined the sound of window blinds being released, spreading along strings. Sadness was a drug, to be mixed with drugs until we couldn't tell what came first, the rain or the lake. Summer had a timer on it. It would end when my dad came back, and then I'd have to start over, and not in the perfect light-filled room on the top floor.

I was at the coffee shop, pretending to read a book instead of watching the door until Mickey walked through it. The entirety of a Radiohead album and a few other songs had played when he finally did, but with a blonde girl wearing a white halter dress.

They sat together at another table. The girl was pretty and also rough, lipstick bleeding onto her watery face. She talked animatedly as he stared at his own hands. Each second passed like a cigarette butt pressed into soft skin. I hadn't planned where to go next or how to get home if nothing happened, or something worse. I finished my coffee and got up to walk outside and take a breath.

"Hey, little girl. Where're you off to?" said Mickey. He reached forward and touched my wrist. His fingers were calloused and warm. I stopped and backed up, the antithesis of this girl with him, a half-deflated balloon on a string.

"Just to the store right there. I heard they don't ID."

"Yeah, they do," said the girl. A woman, really.

"Sit down," said Mickey. "Stay a while. This is Sadie."

"I'm Mickey's confidante," she said, lighting a cigarette, barely moving her mouth.

"She's my landlady," he said. "Let's lynch 'er."

"Shut the fuck up or I'll evict your ass."

"That's her place we were at the other day."

I was happy he remembered. "How was the party?"

His eyelids fluttered.

"The fuck's she talking about?" said Sadie.

"Stephen had people over," Mickey drew out each word. "We didn't trash your house, psycho."

"Better not have. I have things the way I like 'em over there, finally. No more total fucking wrecks living there anymore. Wait," she looked dramatically to one side and blew smoke. "Obviously Stephen didn't invite me to his party, that asshole."

"It wasn't a party," said Mickey. He dropped his head all the way backwards.

"Exactly what I don't like to miss," said Sadie. "Wait," she breathed smoke out again to her side. "How old are you?"

"Fifteen," I said.

"Damn, Mickey, I knew you liked 'em young, but," more smoke seeped out of her mouth. "Whatever. Can we blow this popsicle stick? I don't get why you're always here. You can't even drink here. Oh, shit," she looked at me. "It's all making sense now."

"I don't care for bars," said Mickey in a higher register. "Let's mix something up at home."

"I fucking hate bars. They remind me of work. But a girl's gotta drink."

"Well."

"I got something left over from last night, I think. She coming?"

I looked at Mickey, forgetting that I was physically there and not watching a play. "Come on, one drink," he said.

Sadie led us the two blocks to her house and inside, to a dark dining room that sounded of dragging metal-legged chairs. She pulled on a ball chain hanging from the ceiling and a naked bulb sparked white. Her back was bare and soft, the edge of her dress threatening to expose a stripe of elastic lace as she pulled a bottle of tequila out of an otherwise empty cabinet and a lime out of an otherwise empty fridge.

"Got any salt? We can do shots." Mickey's voice was husky.

"No, I don't have salt." Sadie was pacing the kitchen, smoking another cigarette.

"Looks like you got salt right there," said Mickey, pointing to a cardboard can on the counter.

"We can't just use my roommate's stuff. You can't just take her salt, just because you forgot to bring your own." This was possibly echoing another argument.

"What if," I said. The two turned to look at me. The room became thick with silence.

"What if what?" asked Sadie.

"There's salt at the gas station."

"What is she talking about?" Sadie laughed.

No one looked at me. I'd meant we wouldn't have to buy it, that it came in packets next to the hotdogs, but I could no longer speak. The time I walked into a glass door at the mall, red stains in the laundry, bad smells in school bathrooms, it all clouded over me.

"We don't need salt," said Mickey. He looked at me. "Right?"

I took a deep breath and nodded. Sadie and I sat on couches that butted up against each other in the living room, which was lit with one tall lamp. "Got a smoke?" Mickey asked, walking in with a tray of sliced limes and full glasses. I thought Sadie was going to freak out again. Instead, her eyes glazed over. Without looking back, she reached behind her and opened a small drawer in an end table, the kind of drawer a grandmother would use to store coasters and tea candles. Out of it, she retrieved a blank cigarette from a loose stack. "To Friday," said Mickey.

"It's Wednesday." Sadie had a job, so she had to keep track of days, she said. She was a stripper ("not a dancer, that's bullshit") at Tropics, or what she called Delusions. "There's the gay bar, Diversions, and the gay coffee shop, Discussions, and then there's the straight bar, Delusions," she said. "Come on, that's funny," she added quickly, before we could laugh.

We did the shots, which burned going down and wanted to come back up. My eyes watered. Sadie smacked her lips, sighed loudly and quickly, then stood up. "It's nice out," she said. "Right?"

We followed her back outside and sat on the stoop.

"Beer," said Sadie, even though there was more tequila. I could get carded if I went with them to the store, she decided, so she and Mickey went without me. I sat on the wooden stoop, watching them head out onto an empty street and turn the corner.

Sheila's diaries still sift through me, animating dreams and informing dialogues. I sometimes say, "As my mother said," as if the things she wrote were idioms she repeated, aloud, to others. There were names of friends I'd never met, movies she watched after I was in bed. I want no extra information, only her versions of these things.

If I ever meet a man that she secretly dated, I will see the way he has aged when she hasn't, smell his old breath. Instead, when I read and reread these words, I'm transported to rides that I now know took twenty minutes—drop-offs at the dentist or the YMCA summer program—but felt like hours, commutes during which I'd drift off and have half-waking nightmares about where we were heading.

He's more understanding than I give him credit for. He's making sense of me. He's better at giving me orgasms than anyone else has ever been.

As I learn it, I still can't get this lesson right: drugs and drink are taken to lean toward death. There is no tipping back toward birth or expanding inside a moment, only inching closer to the end. When I see a man bent over on the sidewalk, balancing in the shape of a question mark, it is a reminder that drugs are meant to be fun. In fact, it is the only thing they should be. But, when I'm noticeably high, I wonder if uneasiness, not fun, is the idea. To detach oneself from life because it is so uncomfortable to be there. To put on head-phones in the car, to wear sunglasses in the dark, to bake skin and eyesight red in the sun. To feel the pull of oblivion instead of the hard seat of every day.

In a patch of muddy grass under a streetlight, an ant moved, or a shadow crawled, or a part of my eye couldn't see. Dirt crunched under someone else's shoes. Someone sat beside me, not Mickey or Sadie. He or she seemed some cross between the two, as if they had combined and then returned, ready to tell me a supernatural truth about their relationship. This person was thinner than Mickey and not as bouncy as Sadie, in fact they were impossibly thin, a scarecrow.

"Is this where you live?"

I kept my head down, sensing their face was an empty hole. The voice that came from it was not masculine or feminine, not young or old. It could have come from a machine or a parrot or a folk song.

"I've been to this house before," it said.

I nodded.

"I'm not trying to get you to leave."

I shook my head.

"You'll have fun, I'm sure."

I nodded again.

"All I'm saying is, do you have a dollar?"

I shook my head.

"Gotcha. Right." The voice became increasingly distant. "I believe that. You don't have a fucking dollar, yeah, but you're sitting here making our neighborhood what it is."

Sadie's laugh cut the air. She was holding a tall can of Coors Light half covered by a brown paper sleeve. She walked past me, so

I stood up to go inside. Mickey lit a cigarette and handed it to me, then lit one for himself. He had come back with more energy. "Here," he said, "check it out."

He'd picked up a small suitcase full of tapes from an abandoned yard sale. The neighbors were too lazy to take in their own stuff. I held the case in one hand by its plastic handle, the cigarette in the other. We walked inside together and joined Sadie at the kitchen table. My sight was obscured by a round, red blur. Mickey would pick up a tape and either set it down, saying, "Nice," or throw it out the window, into the alleyway. The Beatles, Journey, Chicago, and the Eagles he threw out. The Rolling Stones, Bob Dylan, and Elvis he kept. Sadie disappeared into a hallway.

"She's all antsy," said Mickey, "because she's off junk."

"Oh," I said.

"Don't touch the stuff."

"Oh."

"It's addictive, you know."

I wondered if the tapes were meant for me, and part of the gift was Mickey weeding out the bad ones. I could listen to them on the bus on the way to school, and they would remind me of my boyfriend who stole them. Sadie came back and said from the doorway that her guy was coming over.

"Your *guy?*" asked Mickey.

"My guy, loser," said Sadie.

This was my new life, starting now.

"Where's she gonna be when he gets here? We don't need nothing extra going on."

"Hey," said Mickey.

I stared dumbly at the tapes, reading the lists of songs.

"Hey."

"Oh." I looked up at Mickey and then at Sadie. The room was dark all around the parts that were directly lit by the lamp. The windows were pitch black.

"Yeah. How are you getting home?"

I had never ridden the city bus and had no idea if there was a nearby stop or if it went to the suburbs or if it ran this late. I could walk to the coffee shop.

"Okay, you can sleep over," said Mickey. He took me into Sadie's room, which was surprisingly clean. I sat on the edge of a made bed. The streetlight lit the pale blue linens through a curtainless window. Mickey left the room and closed the door behind him.

I took my shoes off. I got under the covers with my clothes on. The bed spun. Holding onto the edge of the mattress didn't help. I buried my face in a colorless pillow. Sadie was yelling at Mickey from the kitchen about having to sleep on her own goddamn couch, again, when I could hear the front door open and shut. Another voice appeared, and another. Everyone seemed happy to see everyone else.

When I woke up, Mickey was lying next to me and it was light out. We kissed, his stubble rubbing my cheek as he pulled away. He put his hand on my hip. "I think I'm too out of it to fuck."

"I've never—"

"What?"

"Nothing."

"You've never?" His voice was gravelly.

The word "yeah" rolled out, made of three distinct sounds.

He put his arm across my chest and fell asleep. His dark features were made darker on the clean white bed. Minutes passed and he woke again. He looked at me and sat up, rubbed his face with both hands, and left the room. He and Sadie were speaking to each other in the kitchen. This could be what things are like. An image of my own bed, in the cool basement, throbbed forward. I got up, concentrating on each footstep. Out on the stoop, Sadie, Mickey, and another woman, presumably the roommate, sat while the sun hardened in the sky. Everyone squinted.

"You know what I've always wanted to do to those fuckers?" Sadie was saying. "I wanna take a speculum to work and just put it in there and crank it open and bend over and say, 'Is this what you wanted to see? You like pussy?'"

"What the fuck is a speculum?" asked Mickey.

"You know, right?" Sadie looked at her roommate, who shook her head. "Jesus, haven't you ever been to the gyno? It's what they use to spread you out." Sadie looked at me. "You've probably never been."

I tried to smile.

"You have no reason to." She laughed, looking at each of us, individually.

"Shut the fuck up," said Mickey.

"It's cool," breathed Sadie. "I'm jealous. I bet you go to a real good college."

"No," I said.

"I bet your parents pay for it."

"I'm in high school."

"Mickey." More smoky laughter. "You really do like 'em young." We'd been over this before. She leaned forward and pursed her lips at me. "Which one?"

I looked down. "Crescent Hills."

"Not Dirt City, that's for sure. I went to Rockford, until I didn't. Where'd you go again, Mick?"

"School of Dirt City."

"You didn't go to Rockford."

"Dirtier dirt than that."

"Don't get dirtier than Rockford," Sadie put on a hillbilly accent.

"Shonie."

"I don't know about Shonie being dirt, Mick."

"Enough," he pretended to be incensed. "Dirt City is a state of mind."

Sadie followed a beige sedan with her head as it parallel parked. A gray-haired man in a T-shirt that stretched across a potbelly emerged. "Would," said Sadie. He bent back into the car to get a stainless-steel reusable mug, showing loose-fitting olive cargo shorts. "Absolutely would."

"You wouldn't," said Mickey.

"That's my type, I swear."

Mickey squinted at the man. He reached a hand behind him and squeezed my knee. "Coffee?"

On the walk to Tate's, I felt Mickey's eyes on me.

I touched my hair, a mess. A pocket of my jeans was inside out. We sat at a table near the front, and he brought us two mugs of black coffee, his movements abbreviated, part of a play about our pretended domesticity.

Mickey had to get going, he said, and then, "Did you mean what you said before, about me? I could be your first?"

I nodded.

He squeezed my shoulder. "They'll let you use the phone here," he said, and then took his last gulp of coffee, set the mug down, and swooped through the front door.

Hours later, Robert's car crept into view. He had reluctantly agreed to pick me up after I'd made a few calls to find Candy. She was in the front seat, crawling around it to hug me. I told her about Dirt City first. I would work my way backwards. "I think it means any small town," I said. "Maybe Ypsi counts."

"Lansing definitely doesn't," Candy sneered.

"Does Grand Rapids?" asked Robert.

"No way," said Candy. "It's the second largest city in the state. Are you kidding?"

"I guess I'm not from Dirt City, then," Robert grinned into the rearview. He had to go to therapy, he announced, dropping us off at the apartment complex. "I love you," he said to Candy, and then kissed her, his hands still holding the wheel. Her eyes stayed open, one of them focused on me.

Cassie opened the apartment door because she could hear us in the hallway. "You look pretty," she said, and I felt myself blush. Candy's nose wrinkled and the compliment turned into something else. I wasn't a child. Cassie was the type to say someone was a Christmas baby if they were born near Christmas, or a cusp baby if they were born on the cusp of two astrological signs, and we hated this idea, that a person could say "I'm a baby" and it meant that they were born.

I sat on the counter in the kitchen as the girls each opened a can of tuna fish.

"Mickey," Cassie repeated. "Didn't he used to be—"

"Homeless," said Candy.

"He's staying with this girl Sadie," I said.

"Sadie? What ever happened to her?"

"She works at Tropics."

"Jesus. They all hung out with that kid Ian, Can."

"Ian was my biggest crush. The biggest crush I ever had," said Candy. "He was our neighbor." She was almost yelling now. "I'd love to have sex with him. He said to call him any time, and I never did, because of Robert. Me and Robert had sex last night," she took a bite of the sandwich she'd made for herself. "Twice."

"Stop," said Cassie.

"I would cheat on Robert with Ian."

"Can, don't say that," said Cassie. "Robert is good to you." They got into a screaming match about who knew better that Robert was good to Candy. The phone rang, and I answered it. Norma asked for me, confused. "It's me," I said.

On the after-episode of *Grosse Income*, only Rachel and the host sat on the stage. "Without giving too much away, would you say a lot has changed since you filmed the show?"

"So much. A one-eighty, I'm telling you. My book, my business, everything."

"Since this episode aired, you and your husband have separated. Do you want to talk about that?"

"It's been hard, but it's been a growth period for both of us and you know what? We're better friends now. Never say never."

"You were facing allegations from Patricia that your husband has business ties with Syria. Do you think it was fair of her to bring that up at a party?"

"I—I don't. But you know what? To each their own. I don't know why she has to come up with these crazy stories. And that's what they are. They're crazy. You don't understand; if you knew my husband, you would know that there was just no way."

"Patricia did not invite you to her charity event. It's an amazing charity, it—"

"That, I want to address." Rachel looked into the camera instead of back at the host. "That charity event wasn't hers to invite me to. I was actually invited by another sponsor, and I couldn't attend due to prior engagements." She said these last words as if she was teaching them to a child.

"Hold that thought. We'll be right back."

A commercial for a drug listed its side effects: an increased risk of heart disease, tiredness, trouble breathing, constipation, depression, mood swings, fainting spells, death in some cases. It was unclear what the drug prevented or fixed. A woman walked through the opening of an automatic glass door, holding the hand of a child. Did drugs always have commercials? What side effects would my antidepressant be mandated to list? How would its benefits be played out? A woman being yelled at by her boss and not minding. Laying in the grass for hours. Making the sound of laughter because everyone else was having fun. Mopping the kitchen until it was dark outside, and the rest of the family had gone to bed.

"Now, when we were filming, we didn't know that your friend, who is in at least one episode, was running for local office."

"Absolutely, he is. We've been friends with the Vandenbergs for ages. We've got a sign in our yard," Rachel pressed one index finger onto another, counting one. "You name it," she concluded.

"Is he—are they—distancing themselves, now that—"

"Come on. If there was something to hide, on either of our parts, they wouldn't have agreed to be filmed."

The office was empty, but the computer's dial tone, clicks, and chimes were slams and wails when isolated.

Dominic ran in and looked at the screen. "Hi," he said.

"I'm busy," I said.

"Me too." He bounded down the stairs.

I had only one email, from my old friend, Mari. She always forwarded me chain letters. Each paragraph was separated by dozens of forward-facing arrowheads, indicators of the accumulated number of senders, like dog-eared pages in a used book.

The story was about a young woman who lived at home with her parents and the family dog, a large German shepherd she had known for years now, with warm, trusting eyes. The dog, Shep, guarded the family against hypothetical intruders and other fears, went camping with the trio in summer, and happily chased sledding children in winter, sometimes even worrying neighbors when their kids, who sank into snowbanks as a joke, gave Shep enough alarm to bark until everyone was reunited with his or her parents.

The young woman was getting ready to leave home for college. The Sunday morning before her big trip, she was in her bedroom, drying her hair after a shower, and noticed that the door was slowly opening. Shep hardly ever climbed the stairs to the second floor, so his presence at first surprised her. He walked into her room deliberately and stared at her. His amber eyes and slow pant made her smile. He must know I'm leaving, she thought, and told him to break the rules of the house and get up onto the bed with her so she could hug him goodbye.

He pounced onto the bed with her, pacing happily. His body was heavier than she'd anticipated, and the bed cratered where he stepped, gathering her in its center, his paws catching on her towel. Soon she was in the awkward position of having to escape off the bed from under her dog's muscled legs or hug him naked, her towel now completely balled beneath her. She scolded him by saying his name but found that her voice had gotten quiet.

Shep's tongue hung from his snout, its thin, soft edges propped on rows of sharp teeth. A sympathetic whine emanated from his face without any of his features contracting. He looked into her eyes and stepped again from side to side with his front paws, rocking her naked body and moving his head back, as if to get a better view of her. At this point she was paralyzed with curiosity. She had never seen her dog stare at anyone for so long. She asked him what he wanted, half-believing he would tell her.

Instead, he slipped his tongue back into his mouth, issued a very quiet "ruff," and pointed his nose down. Before she could move or react, his tongue was out again, this time steadily lapping between her legs, first gently, almost questioningly, then with purpose, reaching inside and caressing outside, almost kissing it with the folds of his velvety mouth, letting drool sink into it and slide out.

Now she was paralyzed with pleasure. She was not a virgin, but her high school sweetheart had never gone down on her, and if he had, she was positive it would not feel like this. Shep was diligent and sensitive, looking up at her as he licked, his front legs now flat against the mattress. Within minutes, seconds maybe, she was coming. She scooted up, away from Shep's tongue. He whined again and leapt to his feet, letting her escape the bed. She hugged him, too happy to be ashamed. She had never had an orgasm that good before.

Her legs shook as she walked to her closet, trying to clear her mind by looking for something to wear. She held on to the door as a spell of dizziness took over. She slowly kneeled, not knowing what else to do until the feeling subsided. She felt another lick, this time on her shoulder, and turned to push Shep away, but was met with the sight of his erect penis, red and pointed and glistening with excretion.

The story continued, with a few more sex scenes: in the bedroom, the dog mounted her, and then got stuck inside of her, so she had to wait until he finished before she could move. In the bathroom, the dog followed her and had sex with her again instead of letting her shower, but this time, she loved it and didn't want it to end. She told all her friends, her boyfriend, and her parents how much she would miss them when she went away to college, but in her heart, she knew that the hardest part would be to leave Shep and their blossoming romance. She loved him and would never stop. The secret tortured her for the rest of her life. *Warning*, the email said, *if you are reading this, the story will come true to you unless you pass it along to ten people. If you don't, that means you want it to.*

I didn't respond to the email. I would forward it to ten people. I tried to make a list. I could not send this to anyone I knew. If I couldn't send it to ten people, I shouldn't bother.

I still think about this email and what it would mean if the curse came true.

I wondered if Mari hated me now, too. I wondered if I would see any of my old friends again, or if I even wanted to. It's strange to think about that now, because I ended up transferring back that year and finishing high school in Ypsi. I never got to live in that perfect bedroom with all the windows. I enrolled at Eastern, then dropped out and moved to Chicago to live with my friend Alyssa, who had gotten into Columbia.

Through the internet and visits for weddings, I know that Sadie is a single mom and 200 days clean, that my cousins are making enough money to build their own McMansions and can't handle their liquor on weekends, that Norma and John are divorced, that Lauren didn't graduate, but she did leave Grand Rapids.

Most of my classmates from that year are still there. Some who weren't initially friends became drinking buddies with one another; those with the strongest bonds had falling outs; none of the cliques I once knew are still discernable. Still, when I run into someone about whom I can remember nothing other than their first and last name, the conversation is about the time I knew them better.

Talking with Candy on the phone has become a measurement of our growing differences. When we text, we reminisce. How stupid we were then, we say, ignoring that we are each still stupid, in the same and other ways. Ignoring that what I'd felt for her was more than friendship. I have an easier time keeping up with my best friends from before and after Candy. I have never been good at keeping in touch with exes.

Candy's father was a social guy, always going to karaoke bars, comedy clubs, and theme nights at his favorite "watering hole," so, we figured, if he understood anything, it was the draw of public functions, and we were right. He dropped us off at the coffee shop when we said it was open mic night.

Ian had a blond buzz cut and frosty blue eyes. He was traditionally attractive, which surprised me, because Robert was not. Mickey, who was sitting with him, looked small in comparison to Ian. Sadie was with them.

"Oh shit, no way," said Ian when he saw Candy. He got up from his seat to hug her and there was something adult about that. I said hello to Mickey, trying to read him. He looked incredibly tired. We all sat down, and I tried to pay attention as Ian and Candy caught up, gossiping about people they both knew. Mickey finally kicked my feet under the table. This was the way it was supposed to happen. The night wore on, and Candy's dad was picking us up in thirty minutes, unless she could call him to say we got a ride from someone else.

Ian had a car. "Don't your place got a pool?" he asked.

The car was the color and texture of a shark, and its cushions were spewing yellow foam in the back, where I sat with Mickey and Sadie, since Candy called shotgun and ran for it. When Ian started the engine, the oldies station buzzed on, a tinny version of a song I'd heard a million times but never so flat and far away. The glow of the radio was pretty, too, yellow made by an old bulb or old plastic. The inside of my mouth was a solid chunk.

Candy gave Ian directions to her apartment complex. The boys and Sadie waited in the car as we got out and ran upstairs to check in with Candy's dad. When we opened the door to their apartment, he was asleep on the couch.

Ian, Sadie, and Mickey had already hopped the locked gate to the pool by the time we were back downstairs and outside. Candy shimmied over easily. I clenched my teeth and felt sweat on my temples, hoping no one could tell my legs were shaking. When I reached the other side, everyone was peering into the half-lit water, not at me.

Ian dipped a foot in. "Not too bad," he yell-whispered.

Mickey was the first to take his shirt off. He looked older when he did, but with less tattoos than I had imagined. They were only on his arms. Maybe it was more common to have concentrated clusters instead of an evenly distributed map. Sadie unbuttoned her shorts. I was seeing a stripper strip. It wasn't sexy, really. She rushed the T-shirt off and then stood with one hip out, sucking in and pulling her chest up. Her underwear was black and lacey and matching. Candy pulled her clothes off like I'd seen her do a hundred times. She pulled at my stupid little slip dress. Compared to them, my body would look like a boy's. I was wearing boring white panties and a gray bra with no underwire that said Calvin Klein in block letters across the band. I folded and unfolded my arms. Everyone was strangely quiet. Then Candy and Sadie dove, one after the other, piercing the pool.

Mickey took my shoulder with one hand and reached for my crotch with the other. He started rubbing, hard, and kissing my mouth. He made a sound like he was surprised by the flavor of my lips. He tasted like tobacco. He grabbed at each shoulder and then each bicep and then under my arms and my hips and butt, breathing heavily. Then he pulled away and looked at me.

"There anything going on in there?"

"Yes." I thought he meant my head.

"There're people in the apartment?" He pointed again to the building.

"Oh. Yeah, no. We can't go in there."

"I got an idea," he said. He pulled me by the arm, my dress on the ground but my sneakers on, and led me back to the gate. We had to jump the fence again, this time with our bodies exposed. "It's okay," he said, guiding me behind a wiry bush. He pulled off my underwear and then unfastened my bra with a movement like a snap. I could feel warmth from his pants as he propped me onto him, over the top of his jeans.

I was straddling him, which was the only way, since we were on hard dirt under a terrible bush, but I wanted more than anything to lie down. He unbuttoned his jeans, and his erect penis was out in the open, but I only knew that because he placed my hand on it. Its skin was baby-soft. With another expert move, he placed me onto it by lifting and dropping my hips. My knees dug into the dirt. I tried to move onto my feet, but he pulled me forward and, holding me steady with one hand and himself steady with another behind him, he thrust into me so fast that my whole body lurched. This couldn't possibly be the reaction he wanted. He seemed frustrated with my limpness and slipperiness.

"Is it blood?"

"I don't think so," he asserted. I wanted to sit upright, but with every thrust I doubled over. I had to hug him to get straight. He leaned back and I fell forward. He took each of my arms and straightened them, planting my hands on the ground on either side of his head. He took my hips again and held them still while I braced myself as best I could. He pushed his hips into mine again and again until he pulled out. I could see, in the small amount of moonlight that found us behind that bush, a thick liquid on his stomach.

He let out a long breath and looked up at me. I couldn't see his face in the dark. "Want to get up?" he said.

I stood and watched him duck out into the clearing, buttoning his pants and catching the semen with his hand. He flicked his wrist, and it shot into the dewy grass, which looked soft now, as I dusted off my knees and palms. I stood shakily on one leg, then the other, and by the time my underwear was back on, Mickey was across the field.

None of what was on me was dark enough to be blood. It would wash away in the water. I was sore, but it was outer pain, not a cramp inside like I'd heard about. I was thirsty. I limped to the pool, no longer a virgin.

"Fuck you, fucking little cunt," Sadie was yelling at Candy when I climbed the fence a third time. Ian had circled Candy with his arms from behind.

"No one fucking talks to me like that. Ian, I'm fucking out of here."

"You gotta find a ride, then, I guess, or calm down," said Ian.

Sadie was gathering her stuff. "What's the fucking address here?"

Candy recited her own address, bouncing and splashing.

"You're lucky I'm not in the mood for some shit," said Sadie, who was out of the water and grabbing her clothes from the cement. A cell phone fell out of her pocket, and she bent to pick it up. She hopped the gate beautifully as someone on her speed dial answered and she recited the address of the apartment complex. I could hear her laughing in the distance a few seconds later, and then she was gone. The parking lot, from where we were, was foggy or swarming with bugs.

Ian, sitting on the edge of the pool with both legs in, suggested we all go inside the apartment.

Candy checked while we waited in the hallway. "Coast is clear." Her father had woken up and taken himself to bed, apparently. His door was closed. Cassie was spending the night at a friend's. We were in the bedroom, with two beds and two boys.

Candy and Ian took Candy's. It felt strange to not sit down on it, too. Mickey seemed perfectly comfortable sliding onto Cassie's, shoving the stuffed animals to the ground. "Come here, babe," he said. I had always wanted to be called "babe," and had never told anyone that. I climbed up and knelt over him and he pulled me onto him.

I looked at the other bed. Candy was lying on her back, already undressed again. Ian was arched over her, taking off his shirt. They were backlit by the moon's glow in the small window behind them, but I could see Candy's parting lips and her hands reaching for his fly. Unintentionally, my lips parted at the same speed. I looked back down at Mickey, who was undoing his own pants.

"Want to suck that?" he whispered.

I leaned down and put my mouth around his penis, trying not to move my teeth while I waited for more saliva to materialize. I moved my tongue and he breathed out heavily.

Everything was dark and quiet, but then I heard: "Sup, Mickey?" and two male laughs. I heard Ian say, "Wanna switch?" and Candy say, "Hey," and maybe slap his arm or chest. I heard

Mickey say, "Nope," which made me happy and at the same time sorry for Candy because she would probably not want to have sex with Mickey anyway, but she didn't get to say that first.

I took off my dress. I tried to take off my underwear in a sexy way but ended up rolling onto my back and letting him grab at them until they were caught on my feet and then thrown to the ground. I couldn't think up another way of doing things. There were so many parts to having sex that could not be explained before I'd tried it, parts that were not specific to sex, but to being this close to another person. I didn't know where to put my legs or how to make myself lighter or how to move faster while staying seductively calm. My neck was getting sore.

I thought of the dog story: their bodies are better equipped for fucking, it said. How much of sex was about looking sexy, and how much of it was about fast movements? From this position, all I cared about was how I appeared to everyone else. I thought about kissing Candy. I tried to see her, behind Ian, and could see that Ian was looking at my naked body. He had a better view of me than he had of anyone.

"Damn," he said. I moved faster. Candy was beneath him, probably looking at me, too. I saw Mickey smiling, down there in the darkness. He nodded up, telling me to go ahead, look back at the other couple. I did, and Ian was moving at the same rate. He had a V-shaped torso with toned arms and reservoirs on either side of his belly button that funneled down to Candy, whose legs were almost on either side of her head. Ian was holding them there with both hands. He turned towards me with his chest, and I could see a thick black swastika the size of a tennis ball tattooed over his heart.

My father eventually saved me from it, and so I had to forgive him for leaving me in Grand Rapids for so long. But by the time he came to get me, he was taking me away. Falling back in with my old friends was easy physically. I rode a bike with my old legs, let them take me to the houses I used to visit, where I would push myself onto a countertop with the heels of my hands to listen to a mom talk as she made dinner, lie down on the leather sectional that still made me feel as small as a cat and watch MTV, look out the front window to watch the neighbor mow his lawn.

But nothing was the same, really. Conversations drifted past me; I wanted to change the channel. We didn't go to Hash Bash because we never had. I started to tell stories about Grand Rapids in the same way that I had told Candy stories about Ypsi, giving each anecdote a real ending. Someone had to die or go missing or brush fame.

I talked about "the Calder," a piece of public art that was really named *La Grande Vitesse*, which means *the Grand Rapids*, and how proud of it we were, how its silhouette was on our city flag, even though those were things I learned later. When I first saw the red sculpture, I either thought nothing of it, or that it was an eyesore, it's hard to remember now. I do remember it was used as a meeting point once. I said to my old friends that my new friends would hang out under it all the time. They believed everything I said, or they didn't let on otherwise. I knew that they felt sorry for me because of my mom. That was the biggest thing that had happened while I was gone, so everything else was related.

By then, my father had become something like an acquaintance, and for the rest of my time in high school, we spoke to each other as such. He got a little house close to where we all used to live and dropped me off in his Toyota Camry before driving about an hour to his new job at Pfizer Global Supply. We hardly talked about Sheila, and we never talked about his work. Instead, we became friends, slowly. He sometimes even asked me for advice.

"Do you think I should be dating more?" he'd say.

"Are you dating at all?" I'd respond.

"Ouch. Hey now."

The better I got to know him, the harder it was to imagine my mother ever having loved him. I never said it, but I loved him, and he never said it, but he must have loved me, or else he would have gone to live in Rochester, where worked, instead of bringing me home, to where I could cling to some idea of comfort.

When I moved out, I helped him pack his stuff so he could move, too. He kept his paperwork in bloated manila envelopes stood on end. Each of their metal clasps lay flat and had never been folded. It was one of the many small differences between us. I bent and unbent each of those little arms until they broke off. A corded phone was in a carboard box under the desk. When I knocked over a tin can full of carpenter's pencils, I noticed that it had been hammered by the pencils' tips over time. It was label-less and clean, anonymous other than a sharp lip from a dull opener and those pixel-like dents. I pictured him on his phone, reaching for a pencil to take down some directions, and coming back with a cut thumb. I threw the can away. Sitting on that linoleum floor and putting those pencils into a box, loose, all the times I'd missed him and the absence, now, of Sheila, pulled into one throb.

We went downstairs and into the parking lot to smoke. Mickey, Candy, and I sat on a wheel stop and Ian sat on the hood of his car. I kept looking at Candy to get an idea of how she felt about the tattoo under the T-shirt. She had known this person since childhood, but then again, had not seen him in years.

The two of us had once watched a movie about skinheads that explained how they started as a movement with intentions of revolt, an organized gang that hated the government because it was unfair to its hardest workers. Some of the first skinheads were immigrants, the characters said, which was how their music came to be so eclectic. Soon, though, the group's motives were defined by feelings of nationalism and anti-immigration, then blatant racism. They wanted a stance more viable than the other punk groups of the time who stood for anarchism and drug abuse, and so they became straight edge, clean shaven, and militaristically violent. The overriding image the world later saw of skinheads was the neo-Nazi sect.

One of the mix CDs Candy made me was almost all Motown music. She said that every artist we liked had started out listening to this tiny community, who had recorded in a tiny house, that you could still see as a tourist in Detroit. In the house was a funnel-shaped hole in the ceiling, into which people would sing. It was the most impressive thing about Michigan, she would often say, this hole.

She was interested in anyone misunderstood. The way we were all made to go to the pep rallies and to repeat lies about the school being a place about which we cared deeply was a form of brainwashing, she said. Oppression, like most things, was relative. Candy and Robert lit her copy of *Anthem* on fire instead of returning it, opting to pay the fine. Her teacher assumed she liked the book so much she wanted to keep it.

"She's a capitalist," said Candy, about Ayn Rand.

"Aren't we all?" I didn't mean it to sound like a joke. In my English class, I'd read *Fahrenheit 451*. "Do you have any sympathy for her?" I'd asked Candy. "It was hard for women back then."

"Do you have any sympathy for Candy?" Robert had interjected. "It's hard for women now."

Finally, Mickey said something about the tattoo. "I thought you were going to get that covered up, man."

"It's on my to-do list." The real reason to get rid of it, he said, was the disagreements it kept causing. He never believed in what Hitler said, but in the power that individuals derive from symbolism. It was a statement about propaganda. "We're living in a reactionary society," he said. "I was trying to get a reaction." Candy let smoke seep from her mouth slowly, blank faced. I was sure she was stuck on what Ian said earlier about switching.

"I'm breaking up with Robert today." Candy was awake before me, which never happened. She was sitting up on her mattress, holding her knees. I got the feeling she hadn't slept.

"Are you going to tell him?"

"I hope he doesn't have a nervous breakdown. He's a very nervous person. He was so good to me."

"You can just not tell him about Ian."

"Are you kidding me? I would never tell him about that. People who tell their boyfriends that they cheated on them are self-centered."

"I wonder if Ian will tell anyone."

"I told him not to, and Mickey better not. You better tell him not to say anything."

I said I would tell him that, but the truth was I still didn't have a way to reach him other than running into him at the coffee shop. I wished he could have spent the night so we could go there now together and get a coffee. If a newspaper was there, we could each read a section.

Candy sat very still and stared at the wall. I sat up and for the first time, I leaned in and kissed her. She pulled back and I leaned in again and kissed her bottom lip, and then she touched my forehead with hers. We were breathing audibly, and then in a moment with no beginning, we were in each other's arms, crawling up one another's bodies, nothing like what we'd done with our male partners the night before. She held my face and peered into my eyes, not happy or miserable but intense, and I fell back into the bed. We took turns touching one another, guiding the other's hand or mouth or waist, sighing uncontrollably and then in controlled gasps, each striking a perfect balance until we were each, one and then the other, ecstatic.

"You seem content today," said my therapist, Dr. Herman. He looked at his appointment book. "Did something happen in the past . . . two weeks?"

"Kind of." I hadn't decided what I would tell him yet. "I kind of got a, like, a boyfriend."

He smiled. "Can you tell me about this person?"

"He's in a band. He lives downtown. He's older than me."

"Has he met your family?"

"No."

"Have you spoken to your mother about it?"

Tears jumped up and blurred my vision. "What do you mean?"

"I meant your aunt."

"No."

Dr. Herman sipped from a metal thermos, and I could hear ice rattle inside it. He scrunched his nose so that his top lip was pulled into an M shape, baring his teeth.

"How much older?"

"He's twenty-one."

"Yes, that's a bit older, isn't it? You're how old now?"

"Fifteen."

Dr. Herman's eyebrows rose and stuck there until he started talking again. "That's a big difference at your age. Did you meet him through work?"

"I don't think he has a job." The more I said, the less I knew about Mickey.

"A boy that age. You're a beautiful young girl. I'm sure lots of the boys in school have asked you to go out."

"It's summer break now."

I looked at my hands, which were tightly holding each other. I tried to think of the best way to tell this old man what kinds of people were the ones who got asked out in high school. How it made sense for me to date someone else. He should already know this now, though. The silence became a long one.

"Are you thinking about how your mother would feel about this?"

I was not, strangely. I had no point of reference, no way of knowing how she would feel about anything like this. I had no reason to believe she would approve of me dating someone older, a dropout, a couch surfer, but I had no reason to think that she wouldn't. All I knew was that she wished she weren't married to my dad, cheated on him with some guy named Curtis, hated how trivial it all had felt in the end.

"What about the last thing we discussed." He was looking at his notes. "How you feel about being part of a youth group at church?"

"I'd just rather not."

I called Candy when I got home.

"I couldn't do it," she said.

"Do what?"

"Dump Robert. I love him."

In the master bathroom, I pulled out the diary from under the sink. A teal blue lighter scuttled out with it. I spun its studded little wheel and was reminded of that cigarette cherry on my forearm. The burn had almost completely healed. There was only a pucker in place of the watery blister.

Another beautiful sunset. Sometimes I don't know how I got so lucky. Martha called to say happy birthday a day early. We talked about planning a trip. Me and Tess, we could go stay with her in California. She would love that.

I rifled around in drawers and the medicine cabinet, not sure what I was looking for. A greening coin didn't really heat up because I couldn't hold it to the flame long enough. Holding the lighter to my skin just put it out. A calcifying drain cover kept catching on fire and then sizzling out but staying cool.

Finally, a metal coat hanger stuck behind the toilet was thin enough to get hot but not so thin it melted. I pictured Norma taking some silk dry cleaning directly into the bathroom once she got it home, trying it on in front of the mirrors that opened to show her from multiple angles, wearing it out and forgetting this hanger here, the one that they gave her, that she would have thrown away instead of saved, if it hadn't been kicked to a hidden corner. It worked like a brand, with its own handle. Once it started to glow red, I pressed it onto my arm, near the first burn. It was as thrilling as that time, only better because I was alone. The pain was too much and then it was cold like before. It became a tingle and then a full body rush. I lost my breath. I pulled the metal away before it fused to the skin. I knew the black and the white of it: one pain replaced another, and then the radiant pain made that first sting seem pure, a place to return. I laid on the bathmat and felt the floor spin.

Everyone keeps telling me to take this illness more seriously. I am thinking positive: I will get better. I will get better.

It took me many years to try dating a woman, and when I did, I understood why I'd been putting it off. It was nothing like being with Candy. It was nothing like being with a man, either, and it made me lonely, through no fault of the woman, who was as demure and sexually uninhibited as I wished I could be, but ended conversations without realizing it, saying things like, "I never really think about that," or "It's fine either way."

I had been holding that card, betting it would be the real me. I'd been using it as protection while dating men, having bad sex with men, pouring my heart out to men I wished would try to prove something for me. When the woman and I broke up, I wasn't ready for what it meant. I was that last person at the party, holding a wine bottle upside down over a glass to find it empty. I called her at crazy hours for weeks after, and she would usually answer, there to talk, but uninterested in getting back together. "I always knew you weren't actually gay," she finally said one night or early morning, with a new flatness to her voice.

Lauren picked me up and we rode through the quaint townships of Ada and Cascade to a straight, narrow road that led to Lowell. Along it, signs for free puppies and firewood were nailed to trees, appearing to be permanent fixtures. There would always be free puppies and there would always be firewood for sale, apples to be picked, the 4-H Club fair, greener grass, fatter cows, and closer trees, so long as we kept driving.

I touched the burn on my arm, expecting Lauren to ask about it. Lowell was a quiet, unassuming town, with swans in the river and a petting zoo with every type of baby farm animal, each one raised by a child. Lauren told me all this, and then said she'd never been there. "I'm just curious about another Dirt City, you know?"

"Another?" I asked.

"Some of my family lives in Rockford." She held the R and squashed the O.

"But you don't," I said.

"I never said I did."

The Antique Mall was across the street from the ice cream shop, which was next to the bridge over the river. "Look," I said, pointing at the swans, but Lauren strode ahead to the converted farmhouse.

Each of the mall's stores was a room made up as if people once lived there: a baby nursery with a crib full of yellowed christening gowns, a kitchen of rusted tea kettles and domed cake tins, a bathroom of shaving kits and glass medicine bottles, bedrooms with dolls and books and roller skates. Lauren found a water-stained wedding dress and held it up to her chest.

"I slept with Mickey," I said.

"No way. I fucked Stephen last night. He's in that band with Stephen, right? We should go see them the next time they have a show. We're like groupies."

Lauren sifted through a crate of records with missing sleeves. "This is mostly garbage," she said. My hands were numb and useless. She found a box of metal boxes that used to contain mints and lozenges. "What's a prophylactic?"

A bald, wrinkled cashier, who we hadn't noticed behind a glass case of jewelry, said, "It's a condom." Lauren laughed with her mouth open. I said, "Ha."

In the next room, a teenaged boy manned one of the cash registers.

"From out of town?"

"How did you know?" asked Lauren.

"Know everyone in town. Easy to tell who's from out."

"What's there to do around here?"

"You found it." He grinned and waited. "And the fair, but it hasn't started. We got a movie theater. It shows one movie at a time." He moved his mouth to one side and looked out the front window. "There's the ice cream shop across the street. Good clean fun."

"What about not-so-clean fun?" asked Lauren.

"Where're you from?"

"Grand Rapids."

"Oh, me and my buddies are headed there tomorrow. We love GR."

"We hate it," I interjected.

"I love Lowell, too." He'd said "love" twice now, so easily. The sound of the word was made with gentle pressures, tongue and teeth and lower lip.

"Why?" asked Lauren.

"Well, for starters it's super safe. Way safer than GR. Bet you guys locked your car when you parked here, didn't you? No one around here does. My friends and I once found a set of keys in the ignition of an unlocked limo."

"Did you steal it?"

"Course not." His eyes were wide. "There're some guys from school that sometimes ditch and break into unlocked houses. They take jewelry and try to sell it here, but we don't really buy anything."

"Maybe people should start locking their fucking doors," said Lauren.

When we left, I decided I liked him, the Antique Mall boy. I hated Lauren, and Stephen, too. My new crush was a crush on a whole other life, a place where Stephen and Mickey would never go. As we drove back to the city, though, the thought faded, along with the greenery and the sky. From Lauren's car window I watched people leaving gray stores with brown shopping bags and sitting at bus stops holding clear bottles. A woman in a two-piece stood in a parking lot, holding the sign for Teeny Bikini's, a new bar. We pointed at her, and at a man in the car next to us who looked transfixed by her.

"It's a condom," Lauren said in a high, eager voice.

I am an adult now, and I don't feel any braver. I will avoid whole neighborhoods due to the memory of an overstayed welcome. Even thinking about certain places, certain streets, I can smell that sharpness of a snorted powder, feel its flavor on my throat, recall saying something I wasn't sure was true.

If you were to ask me what it was that happened in any of these homes, clubs, cars, corners that made them seem so dark to me now, I couldn't easily tell you. Minds are capable of a lot, or of everything, meaning all that we know, and I've intentionally dissolved parts of my brain with chemical shards and liquids, distressing existence's fabrics each time. The day after taking ecstasy, one is, ironically, depressed. It's a bizarre feeling, knowing that sadness is only based on a temporary imbalance, and yet not being able to think one's way out of it.

I've sought stability, in some ways: lower peaks and shallower valleys, maybe. High highs and low lows are the only alternative, I've noticed, and it's a combination of things including cowardice that has kept me from seeking those. I'm afraid, mostly, that I won't be able to believe enough, that I'll look around me and see people acting like children, that all I'll realize is that there isn't much here, that, like a rollercoaster, it's physically impossible to be dropped from anything taller than the starting point.

At the next Blues on the Mall, Stephen was standing against a wall and talking to a group of people at the pavilion. Candy and Robert were in an argument that didn't involve me, so I walked up to him, with nothing to lose.

"Have you seen Mickey?" I asked.

"She's a cop," said one of the guys.

"Mickey?" said Stephen.

I nodded.

"Nope."

A woman with white hair sighed quickly as she edged around me. The sidewalks were less crowded than the street. Surrounding the amphitheater were carts selling tacos, ice cream, and bottled water. Underfoot were blankets covered in bootleg DVDs, cocoa butter, and incense sticks. A carved stone statue of a man with a penis so large he couldn't circle it with his arms or legs sat on a rug.

A Dalmatian-spotted Great Dane sauntered down the street, his owner a middle-aged woman wearing an ornamented hiking backpack. The dog's eyes looked too human. Within a group of boys skating on the steps, I recognized the one from the Antique Mall. It was ridiculous to see him again, the very next day. Maybe I'd seen him many times and never noticed, didn't care who he was until he was right in front of me, behind a counter, forced into conversation. I stopped walking and watched the boys take turns trying to land tricks. A crush pulsed back.

"We're going to the top of that building right now," Stephen said.

I nodded. Candy and Robert had disappeared.

We entered the lobby of a tall building and half-ran to a freight elevator. One person was behind me, the lookout, trailing intentionally. I glanced back and he motioned for me to hurry ahead. When we were all inside the elevator, someone pulled the seatbelt strap handle so that a door rose from below and met one that was falling from above. A loud metal gate crashed down next. Someone asked how Stephen had found out about this place. He pretended he hadn't heard the question.

The black tar roof had low walls around it, on which we could sit, or over which we could fall backwards and drop ten stories to the crowded street. One of the guys lit a joint and passed it around. Everyone was talking too quietly, or there was a ringing in my ears that was drowning them out. Stephen was not talking. It looked like he wasn't listening, either. "Do you know if Lauren is here?" I finally said.

"Who's Lauren?"

I looked right at Stephen, no longer afraid of his eye contact. "Really?"

"Are you lost?" he asked.

"I don't have a cell phone."

"Do you want me to call someone for you?"

"Candy doesn't have one either."

"Who's Candy?"

"Does Mickey have a phone?"

"Mickey. How do you know Mickey?"

I thought about it. "Lauren—"

"Lauren . . . Lauren."

One of the guys moved closer and gave the joint to me. "I know Mickey. I think he's here somewhere."

"Yeah?"

"How old are you?"

"I'm in a band with Mickey," said Stephen, before I could answer. He was standing with one foot on the wall, taking the joint from me.

His fingers touched mine and I dropped it.

"Oops," he said and picked it up before it rolled away. "Butterfingers."

I grabbed at my hair. It was getting whipped by the wind.

"You should come to our show tonight. It's at some warehouse, I don't know."

"What's your band called?"

"Dirt City."

"Dirt City," I repeated.

"Where are you from?"

"Ypsilanti."

"Where Iggy Pop is from."

From this perch, downtown looked vast and varied, with buildings of every height and width, people of every shape. The Grand River churned away, its foam snaking and dispersing at a pace that mocked the waddling crowd. Bridges stretching over it led to another part of the city. I couldn't remember ever having been on a bridge.

When we emerged from the freight elevator back on the first floor, the lookout made sure the coast was clear. Mickey was on the sidewalk, staring at his feet. "I always miss all the fun," he said, and then, to me, "Hey, little girl."

His face was smaller than I'd remembered. "Stephen said you're playing a concert tonight," I said.

"Show."

"What?"

"We're playing a show." Stephen was suddenly gone.

"You dummy, where were you?" Candy's voice came from behind us. "Robert is mad at me. He left."

"Why?"

"Where were you?"

"On a roof with Stephen." I motioned with a shoulder at Mickey.

"And you didn't find me first?"

"I didn't think they would wait."

"If they cared about you, they would," said Candy.

It looked like rain. They didn't care about me, of course not. I hadn't given anyone a reason to. "We can go to a show tonight," I said. "At a warehouse. And take the pills."

"I want to take mine now," said Candy.

As we walked, we took out the Batman baggies and swallowed the Klonopin or whatever it was. A raindrop hit my face.

"Remember me?" Mickey said to Candy.

"I remember your friend Sadie almost got us all arrested. She better not be around."

"She's alright."

"Yeah, I don't give a fuck."

"When is your show?" I asked Mickey.

"Should we get something to drink?"

"Oh fuck," said Candy. "Are you with Ian? Fuck."

"Nope," said Mickey.

"We can't go to a bar," I said. "We took Oxy. Or something."

"No shit, you got more of that?"

"No," said Candy.

"You know the rule is, don't say nothing unless you got some to share."

"That's not a rule."

The remaining parts of the day and that night were only memorable in patches, recognizable characteristics of a landscape that takes shape when you face backwards as the vehicle moves forward. The pills must have had some effect on the way we behaved, but all we could recall was a sense of detachment, like we were watching a movie. We cuddled together in a car. Whose car, we wondered.

Mickey, in the passenger's seat, gave the driver directions. Other men helped with fitting a drum set in the trunk and all around us in the back seat. Metal parts made hollow noises when a pothole was hit. We became tangled piles, limbs distributed around the rods, our mouths wide open and silent. The next stop, maybe, was this warehouse that felt empty even as the band played. We shared a folding chair. We kissed each other, maybe in front of people.

The songs the band played were covers, one being "Sixteen," or maybe "Eighteen," we couldn't remember. When it started, Candy yelled, "We're sixteen," or "We're eighteen," even though we weren't. Either she was told by someone to be quiet, or it was me who told Candy to calm down, or no one said anything, other than a voice in my head. There was an older girl there, and Candy said, "She's jealous," too loudly.

Stephen must have played guitar, and Mickey must have played the bass, and someone must have played the drums, and maybe there were more band members, but we couldn't remember any of that. We stumbled around the building looking for a bathroom and everything appeared as if lit by a searchlight. Candy fell down a set of three stairs and I got worried, but she rolled over and, lying on her back on a rotting wood floor yelled, "I'm okay," and we both collapsed in silent laughter again, hushing one another in the fear that someone would get mad at us for having fun.

We woke up in Candy's bed, surprised to find our hair damp and our clothes still on. In Candy's pill book, a side effect of clonazepam was short-term memory loss. "It was the greatest night of our lives," Candy said to her sister across the room. She had both arms around my waist under the covers.

"Do you remember Dad picking you up at the Liquid Room?" asked Cassie, annoyed. "He said you used the phone there. It was like ten."

We had imagined we were out much later than that, and in a part of town we had never been. To Cassie, we suggested what we might have said to the guys in the band, and to the girl who had tried to get us to shut up. Stephen thought we were cool, for sure. He thought we were funny, at least. He would have said something into the microphone if he had wanted us to leave. Had there been a microphone? Was Sadie there? Was Lauren? Had Mickey wanted me to leave with him?

It was the hottest day of the year. We put on bathing suits and went to the pool. Candy's father came out with two beers for us. "Don't tell the neighbors," he said, even though we were in the middle of an apartment complex, and everyone could look down on us from their windows.

Candy finished hers quickly and threw the can so it hit the metal gate. She hung onto the side of the pool and stared at the cloudless sky through sunglasses. No one else ever came out and swam. I let myself fall back into the water and float. When he came out again, Candy's father brought us hotdogs in buns with mustard stripes. We ate them with wet hands, watching the bread dissolve under our fingertips, dropping what we didn't eat onto the cement rim. When the skin on our shoulders had ripened and was about to peel, we went inside and changed into t-shirts and boxer shorts, then got under a blanket on the couch to watch an episode of *Grosse Income*.

Rachel, Bella, and Patricia are in the back of a limousine. Patricia is explaining something delicately, holding her hands up as if there is a ball between them. Tears dot the corners of her eyes. "It's been hard to keep quiet about this," she says, flanked by the two women, all of them facing forward. "Abuse is not something that you're dying to talk about in public, you know. People don't understand it. They think you're not being honest. They treat you differently. Most people would rather just not deal with everyone knowing. It's too much of a burden. But it's important, to me, to bring this kind of thing to light. It was important that I start a foundation that helps raise awareness and community support, breaking the silence, because it is always painful. It never goes away. It hurts more the longer you don't talk about it."

"Well, I think it's incredibly brave," says Rachel. "It's incredible what you're doing. I started a foundation that is very personal to myself as well, so I know how it makes you feel—"

"Vulnerable," says Bella. "It does; it makes you feel extremely vulnerable, and it is so beneficial for others, whether you feel that or not, to show that side."

"Absolutely," says Rachel.

"And now what we're doing next is creating this tool for victims to use to connect with one another, this software, it's really something, my team is so amazing, the best at what they do. And part of the proceeds will go to the foundation, of course, and it is just going to change everything, I think. It's really, really, so smart."

"You'll have to have a huge launch. One here and one in LA. I could help you with a guest list—you know, we have the hall out there, where we do the wrap parties. We do lots of charity events there, too. Of course, we'd always love to have you."

"Wow," says Bella. "The software isn't even invented yet and you're getting dibs on hosting the party."

"I'm not getting first dibs, that's not what I'm doing."

"The software is very close to being finished," says Patricia. The car makes a sharp turn, and everyone careens to one side, shouting. Rachel holds a bottle of prosecco over her head and says, from the side of her mouth, "Watch it, watch it, we got precious cargo back here."

"It just seems very Hollywood, that's all."

"Listen, I could live in Hollywood if I wanted to—I *should* live in Hollywood—and I don't. What does that tell you about me?" Rachel yells at Bella, who puts her hands up as a shield for potential free-flying saliva. "And what I've always thought about you is that you're a little phony yourself, to be quite honest. And I can smell phony. Your whole homegrown holier than thou act? It's a [bleep] affectation. You think that no one sees through it, but I do."

"You're obsessed with fame. That's already clear. And now you're letting a projection of your own fame go straight to your head," says Bella, calmly. "Let's all take a breath." She stands with bent knees and starts to shakily walk while hunched in half so she can sit on another bench in the car. The camera zooms out to follow her. In a testimonial, she says, "It's sad, really. Some people can't separate what they are presenting to the world and who they really are. I think Rachel needs to have a long talk with her husband, if you want my opinion about it."

"Coming up," says a voice. A clip plays out of context. "There is a [bleep] hierarchy, and everyone else is aware of that," says Bella over a white tablecloth full of crystal glasses. "So, either you're [bleep] stupid or you're playing [bleep] stupid."

During the commercial break, we argued about who was more disgusting: me, for having slept with a junky, or Candy for having slept with a neo-Nazi.

"Ian's very clean," said Candy.

"Mickey doesn't even do heroin," I said.

"Oh, sure."

Cassie came home from work. "At least I'm not cheating on my boyfriend," I said, as she opened the door.

"Who's your boyfriend?" Cassie asked.

"No, I meant—"

"She meant Mickey," said Candy.

"Oh." Cassie bared her teeth and inhaled.

"He's not really homeless," I assured her.

"No, no, no, no, that's not it. It's just that—oh, fuck, I hope I'm wrong about this. I was just at the coffee shop."

"Gross," said Candy.

"I saw him with that girl Lauren."

"Everyone goes there," said Candy.

"No, they were—she was sitting on his lap. But seriously, fuck that guy, you're too good for him," said Cassie, to me.

I stared at the TV screen. The sound was muted. I thought I might throw up.

"I told you Lauren's a fucking slut. Stephen could have been a coincidence, but Mickey was off limits and she knew it," said Candy.

"I don't know," I said. "I don't know." Sometimes it was better not to hear a thing, I thought. Sometimes it was better to forget it right away.

"Unlike you gals, I gotta work tomorrow," said Candy and Cassie's father from his bedroom. "So, tuck yourselves in."

We stayed on the couch for hours longer, my head in Candy's lap. I was hers now, and Candy was going to break up with Robert anyway, because she had to. When we were both single and free from all this awfulness, we would go on a real date, the two of us. It's what we had always wanted. We would go Dutch. She thought that was funny.

Cassie was in the bedroom; otherwise, we would go there. Instead, we went outside again, sneaking some of Cassie's cigarettes out of her purse so we could smoke them in the parking lot. We were sitting on a curb, starting to get cold, then Candy gasped.

"What the fuck are you doing?" she whispered. A figure was walking toward us.

"Wanted to come see you." The voice was Ian's.

"My dad lives here," said Candy, smiling.

"How is that dude?" he asked. "Haven't seen him in a minute."

We sat outside for long enough, and then Ian followed us into the building. He bounded up the stairs and walked ahead of us, as if he knew which apartment was Candy's. She told him. She opened the door with her key, shushing us. The apartment was dark. The refrigerator smacked open, and Ian was illuminated. "Mind if I grab a beer?"

"You have to leave," repeated Candy. "I'm gonna get in trouble."

"Or you can come back with me," said Ian. "Both of you."

Candy needed to think. She needed to go into her room to do this. I didn't need to think about anything, though. The option to leave was always the best one. I pictured Candy and I in the backseat.

"You okay?" asked Ian. He sat on the other barstool and put his hand on my thigh, drained the can of beer, set it on the counter.

"Do I look not okay?"

"You look pretty." Mickey had never said I looked pretty. Ian put his other hand on my other thigh. Candy came out of her room wearing a white sweater over her tank top.

"Tess," she said. "Do not."

"Come here," said Ian. "You can get in on this." He kissed me without warning. He moved his hands around my body and reached back, trying to grab Candy's little wrist. When he stopped kissing me though, Candy was gone. Ian and I were silent, looking in every direction, and then she reemerged from the bathroom, one of her beloved potted plants held high over her head.

"What are you doing?" asked Ian.

She threw it down hard. It hit the carpet with a thud and sprayed soil at a wall. The plant was a tangled mess, its thickest stem torn to expose shimmering insides.

"Candy, wait," I pleaded, but she was out the door and down the hall. Ian and I ran, following her out of the building to the back and over the grass to the pool. She was sitting on the edge, her bare feet dangling in the water already. The gate whined open.

"Not here," hissed Candy, coming to life and almost slipping all the way in. The water lapped and rippled around her. "I live here." My ears burned through to my eyes. Neither of us said anything else. The sleeves of her sweater were soaked.

Ian said, "I'm going on a drive, and I want you to come."

"Where?" I asked.

"Sadie's."

"Fuck no," said Candy. She was looking at me when she said it. I desperately wanted the moment to pass without a decision being made and to be in a car, any car. And then Candy made the decision. "Get away from me," she said, not whispering. "Leave."

I sat in the passenger seat, silently thinking about the kiss, then the swastika tattoo, kiss, swastika, repeating: a chorus and verse. We pulled up to Sadie's, where Mickey was waiting on the porch. I got out of the car on shaky legs.

"Shotgun," shouted Mickey, taking my place up front.

"Oh," I said, and opened a door to the backseat. It wasn't until we were moving again, one of the tapes from the little suitcase inserted into the deck, that Mickey turned around and peered into the empty space around me. "Where's your little friend?"

"There was some drama," answered Ian.

Mickey sighed. "Bad news."

"I've known that family forever," said Ian, not in response.

"Well, the little one is a little nuts," said Mickey. "You gotta admit."

Maybe she was, I thought to myself. There was the time she got sent to the nurse's office for having a fit in the locker room, a story I'd heard described by other girls as "terrifying." There was the time she told me she couldn't see, that she'd woken up without sight, and then silently wept until it came back. There were a lot of times.

I may have fallen asleep and woken up once we were on the highway. I felt exhausted and tense, not sure where we were going and not able to ask. Signs for rest stops flashed by. The headlights picked up a silver guardrail and made striped shadows on carpet-thick pines. "Thirty miles," said Ian, as we passed a sign that said, among other things, "Newaygo 30." I had never heard of Newaygo.

I must have fallen asleep again and then woke up to Ian saying, "She's hot."

"I know she is," said Mickey, "but she's pretty dumb."

I breathed in too loudly.

"Shit," said Ian, laughing. Mickey drank from a pint of Black Velvet and didn't say anything or laugh. Sometimes it was best to forget what was heard instead of figuring out what it meant. We stopped at a gas station and Ian got out of the car.

My friends have revealed that they were hurt as children, that they cannot trust anyone with a way about them like the assailant's. I learn about lifelong afflictions with butterfly effects. When we get angry with each other, these memories are used as blunt forces, crashing into arguments. They are clumsily written, unexpected guests at the door in a thunderstorm, overused and under-protected. And they splinter, get sharper, duller, greased with humor. A story, however old, represents the time in which it is repeated, not the time when it happened. The most painful of circumstances are turned into plot points or left on the cutting room floor. Plain heartbreak is too boring to mention.

"Want anything from in there?" asked Mickey. He was speaking to me, apparently. I did want something, surely, but I would have rather gone into the gas station convenience store with him, looked down all the aisles together.

"Not really," I heard myself say.

He got out of the car and headed across the lot. Ian leaned against the pump. From this vantage point, moth shadows flickering over his face, he looked older.

I'd always loved gas stations, the potential to see inside a relationship. A stop to fill up was an interruption of some longer event, a private conversation. People continued to argue there, in comfortable clothes. I wondered what it felt like to throw a fountain soda at a windshield or refuse to get back in the car as it slowly trailed me.

The men circled, with me reclining in the back seat. It was as if I was still asleep, dreaming in washed out colors. Maybe one day I could be in a car with just Mickey, and we could fight at a gas station. Maybe I would get out, wearing a bright-colored tube top. Maybe he would threaten to leave me there, gripping the steering wheel. I'd stomp off to the store and flirt with the attendant until he followed me in, at which point I'd saunter back out to the car, holding a long piece of stolen licorice. I remembered seeing a pregnant teenager filling up a motor scooter's tank, staring at me in the passenger seat of my mother's Toyota Camry, and feeling sorry for her.

Maybe I seemed dumb because I was quiet. Or maybe I seemed dumb because I was dumb. Maybe the girl who was hot was not me. Ian was tapping the nozzle on the car's metal lip, a sound I'd heard my whole life. Mickey came back inside. It was me and him.

"What if we pretended to be in a fight?" I murmured.

"I don't get it."

"I want to smash a bottle," I said.

"I'm not looking to get arrested. I don't know about you, but I don't want to go back to jail."

"You were in jail?"

"I got warrants."

"How long were you there?"

"A few months. That's a lot of crossword puzzles."

I looked at the back of Mickey's head. "Did you meet anyone interesting?"

"You don't make friends in jail, if that's what you're asking." He lit a cigarette as Ian got back in the car.

"You owe me, man," said Ian.

"Have a smoke," said Mickey, tapping a cigarette out of his pack.

"Can I have one?" I asked, emboldened by our conversation. Mickey gave me his cigarette and lit a new one as we pulled out of the station and onto the highway again.

Was it okay to ask someone what he went to jail for, once he was out? If he was only there for a few months, it couldn't have been that bad. Could someone's death, accidental or intentional, be involved? Maybe death wasn't the worst thing in the world, only the worst thing I'd witnessed. Maybe it would be easier to deal with death if there was more of it around. My mother's biggest regret when she died was that she had not lived enough. Was it better that I didn't know what was at the end of this drive?

I watched Mickey hold his cigarette butt up to the cracked window and release. The night air drew the ember up and away. I held mine up to my cracked window and let go, but the air didn't pull the butt out, it forced it in.

"Get that," said Ian. "Get that, get that, it's gonna burn my car." He craned his neck to look at me and held the back of Mickey's seat. "Can you get that?"

Mickey reached back and found the cigarette rolling around on the floor, still lit. He tossed it out the window, somehow getting the suction just right again.

"Pay attention," said Ian, facing forward and not looking into the rearview. He hit the steering wheel with the heel of his hand.

I didn't know the summer would be bookended with death then, but if I had, I would have thought that one of these boys would overdose. They liked to swing closer to dying than anyone I'd ever seen. Life was a loop, their habits said, not a hill to climb. Knowing that you were already where you would end up was both exhilarating and bleak.

Soon we were taking an exit and then a dirt road. Lights of differing sizes and yellows spread out ahead of us on either side, over doorways of mobile homes with dark windows.

"Which one is it?" asked Ian.

"Here he comes." Mickey rolled down his window. "Man of the hour."

We pulled up to one of the trailers.

"Mine's actually the one out back," said the stranger in the dark. He explained how and where to park as Ian cursed and maneuvered over the dirt, kicking dust into the headlight beams. The stranger jumped in front of the car and gave two thumbs up, smiling as Ian cursed some more, saying he "could kill that motherfucker."

"That's just Doug," said Mickey.

"Welcome to my neighborhood," said Doug, opening the car's driver side door. "It's a little grimy, but it's home." He spoke loudly, piercing the stillness around us. We all got out and slammed the doors shut. The headlights were off, the dust invisible, the dirt grinding under our feet in the darkness. We each stepped up a little metal staircase and into the trailer.

"Newaygo: now, why go?" said Doug, who had yet to introduce himself.

"Better than Bland Crapids," said Mickey.

There was one other guy whose name I never caught, a roommate or another visitor. From inside, the trailer was bigger than I'd thought, with a hallway that looked like it led to a few rooms with doors and a linoleum-tiled kitchen with a little stove range and a sink. We all sat on a brick-orange couch and armchair in front of two metal TV trays. Doug, pretending to be a waiter with a paper towel over one arm, kept getting up to fetch ice for our glasses of vodka and Sprite.

He worked at a Baskin Robbins in town and the other guy worked at the Meijer in Fremont. Newaygo wasn't big enough to have a Meijer. Ian said he would be starting a construction job soon. Mickey didn't say anything, and so I didn't either, in solidarity. It was after midnight, so my next shift at work was technically tomorrow. How long would we be here? We all went outside for a cigarette.

One moment I was sitting on a lawn chair smoking, and the next moment I was standing in the kitchenette. I had no recollection of movement, of climbing those little hinged steps, or of everyone leaving except for Mickey, who was sitting on the couch, staring at his drink. I was standing close to the sink, as if to wash my hands. "Where is everyone?" I asked, my voice far away.

Mickey shushed me without looking up. "People are sleeping. We get the couch." The couch was too narrow to share, though, and we ended up on the hard floor, covered in tapioca-colored carpet. The light on the outside of the door made a bright yellow square around us. I rolled over and hit my head on something. "Ow," I whispered, and then, to fill the silence that followed, "Did Ian leave?"

"Yeah," Mickey drew a breath. "He's not too happy with me."

I found a glimmer of memory, Ian's car creeping away in the lamplight, crunching gravel. Or was that just something I could picture easily? It was too cinematic, the blues and whites and silvers. I could see his expression as bubbles of shadow skated over his face and he drove under the streetlights back to the highway. I could smell the exposed foam of the vinyl seats. Had I been outside on a chair by myself at some point? Mickey fell asleep with his arms splayed and started to snore.

The little suitcase was on the end table. I sat up and opened it. Along with a few of the tapes were a Ziploc bag full of hypodermic needles and a spoon. It was as ugly and familiar as a used condom on a sidewalk, even if I'd never seen it before. In fact, it was uglier, and more familiar. I'd had sex twice now and never used a condom. A prophylactic. I moved onto the couch and draped my legs across one arm while resting my head on the other.

Doug seemed fun. Maybe he was gay. How long had I been standing in the kitchenette? It would be worse if the block of lost memory was full of conversations during which I was not in control of my functions. Maybe now is when I will finally break down, I thought. When I closed my eyes, I did not see black. Instead, I saw the inside of the trailer as if it were on a black-and-white TV show. Parts of it even looked fuzzier and flat, as if on a screen. I opened my eyes again. The room was in color and three dimensions. I closed them again. Mickey sat up. Sighing, he hopped to his feet and walked to the sink. He took a glass from the cupboard and filled it with water.

"Can I—" when I started to talk, I remembered that my eyes were shut. When I opened them, though, Mickey was still asleep on the floor. Was this what I was doing while the others were in a room together? Was I out in the front while the men were inside? I could have been rocking back and forth on a lawn chair, closing my eyes, and talking to people I only imagined were there. I closed my eyes again and Mickey was handing me the glass of water. I wanted water badly now, but I was glued to the couch. My mouth felt like the Tin Man's. "Oil," I said. I opened my eyes. Had I said it aloud? Don't talk. Sleep. My body wrestled itself up and then I was sitting. Lay down. I did. Sleep. I closed my eyes. The scene reappeared and it was daylight there. Mickey was outside but the wall had a window in it big enough to show him sitting there, drinking the water that now had ice cubes floating in it. He smoked a cigarette. The sight of the cigarette made me thirstier. The cigarette was gone. I opened my eyes. No window at all. I stared into a dark corner inside the room. I closed them and the corner was brightly lit and covered in floral wallpaper. This cycle continued for ages, and then I must have fallen asleep, because Mickey was on top of me, and it was morning, and he was trying to get my shirt off.

"Was this your first morning sex?" Mickey's forehead was beaded with sweat.

"I guess so." My body was a bruise.

He got up and took a cigarette out of a pack on the floor. I sensed he was not going to ask me to join him outside, so I said, "My friend saw you with Lauren."

"What Lauren?"

"My friend, Lauren."

"Your friend is Lauren, or your friend saw me with Lauren?"

"Both."

"I know a couple Laurens."

"Are we," I had to pause and remember the correct word. "Are we exclusive?"

"I haven't fucked your friend, if that's what you're asking," said Mickey.

I pulled my jeans up, still lying flat. I looked away.

"In fact, the last time I had sex was with you." He said this almost incredulously. "And I don't mean just now. Or last night."

Last night. Ian was driving away angrily. I closed my eyes and the shark car lurched. I focused on what I wanted to happen next. I wanted to be fully awake. I wanted to not be so tired. I wanted to be washing the dishes in that little sink, looking out the little window. Mickey could come home from a construction job out in Newaygo or Fremont or White Cloud or Rockford or Ionia and see me there, wearing an apron. Maybe we were near Holland, Michigan. I had gone there once to see the tulip festival. Mickey could bring me a bouquet of flowers and kiss me on the back of the head. His arms would wrap around my waist. And that was all. I just wanted that from him.

"Yo," said Doug, coming out of his room. "You guys sleep okay out here?"

"Might need a coffee," said Mickey.

"Don't have any here, but there's a gas station down the street. If you're feeling fancy there's a store, like a, you know, a grocery store, that has a café in it." If Doug was gay, he was probably the only gay person in this whole town. If his home was mobile, he could always move it. His voice filled the room.

My voice was tiny, and only sounds: "oh, uh, huh." I had to make sure they knew I was still there and not stupid or mute or unaware that some grocery stores had cafés in them. I wanted to be spoken to directly, wanted this so badly that it consumed other thoughts about where we were, how we would get home, where I called home and where Mickey called home, if anyone had a phone here, what happened last night.

Doug walked across the living room and opened the front door, a flimsy little aluminum-framed thing that unclipped from the wall. It was like he'd punctured the lid of a can, and now it was apparent that the interior was thick with smoke and dust. "Oh, it's a nice one," Doug yawned, stretching his thin limbs and running his hands down his sides. "We gotta do it, we gotta get out there."

Grassy air stood at the door. Sleep would be wonderful, if it could combine with sunlight and that outdoor smell somehow. I wanted a white, covered comforter and cool, down-filled pillows instead of a nylon blanket and some tweedy cushions. Doug stepped lightly down the steps, which were rungs, and disappeared. The smoke from his cigarette lazed in.

"Want to go for a walk?" asked Mickey. If Candy knew where I was, she would say that she didn't understand what I was getting out of this, but she would be lying. I got up and followed Mickey out the door. The three of us walked along an empty road because there was no sidewalk, only dirt staked with power lines on wooden poles and piles of trash left out of dumpsters in the hopes that someone could make use of the broken things: a toaster blackened around the slots, a curling iron missing its lever, a humidifier still full of water, a sliced-up lampshade showing a red clearance sticker.

I'd been wearing the same clothes for three days. My hair was tangled. Makeup was probably pooling in the corners of my eyes. Passing cars had a view of myself and these men with their scars and stubble and hair-smelling heads, crawling under the sky. A man in an Amish buggy tethered to a pair of horses didn't hide his stare, following us with his whole head. The way to get even closer to the men, I thought, would be to complain.

"I need to find a phone," I said.

"Gotta call your folks?" said Mickey.

"My aunt. She'll be pissed she doesn't know where I am."

"Why doesn't she know where you are?"

"There's a pay phone at the store," said Doug.

"Got any money?" asked Mickey.

I put my hand in my purse and realized all I had there were a few quarters. How would we buy coffee? Mickey said he hadn't gotten to that part yet. He'd used the rest of his cash on cigarettes. No, he didn't have any kind of card, he added before Doug could ask. Doug didn't say what he had or didn't have. No one asked him. We could return some cans and bottles at the store, Mickey suggested. "Save the planet along the way." He smiled at me. I smiled back. I no longer felt tired.

Mickey plucked a grocery bag off a shedding bush. I found another hanging from a tree and placed a wet Corona bottle into it. It was an Easter egg hunt but smelling of hot beer and soda crust. Doug helped with only one hand, the other always holding a cigarette. I dove for a Bud Light can stuck on dried mud that had washed towards a gutter. When I held it upside down, watery liquid shot toward me. I leapt backward and let out an uncontrolled noise, finally making Mickey laugh. He stopped walking and held his knees.

"Come on," I said. I ran for glass sparkling in the grass.

"Wait," said Mickey. He retrieved the bottle from my bag and emptied it of a cluster of wet cigarettes by thudding the bottom with the palm of his hand. He said stores wouldn't take empties with butts or lemons in them, since they mold over. His voice softened. He was thinking about the people who had to sort the returns, the air they had to breathe.

"Dude, it's a machine," said Doug.

The grocery store was about a mile from the trailer, and we had scavenged sixteen bottles and cans between us by the time we got there. A deposit counting machine was in the entryway. We took turns pushing our trash inside. The cylindrical shoot could sense it was being fed and would seal itself over with a small door while it read the spinning vessels and then disposed of them with a satisfying crunch of metal, a collapse of plastic, or a clink of glass. It printed a receipt, for which the cashier at the café gave Mickey one dollar and sixty cents.

With this change and mine, we had enough for two small coffees and a phone call. Even so, Mickey asked the cashier if I could use their phone for free. The woman, charmed by the men and their excitement over the best coffee they had had in "I don't know how long, do you?" said that I could step into the manager's office. He was off that day.

I was led past produce and dairy, through a doorway with a curtain made of rubbery plastic strips situated between beer cooler doors. Behind it, the floor looked like the bottom of an old boat that had been patched with rugs. Stacks of cardboard boxes, some of them filled with Gatorade, flanked another door, which opened to an office, where the woman said I could sit at a desk covered in folders, calculators, and receipts. She picked up the receiver of a beige phone and dialed two buttons before handing it to me and walking out.

Years later, I would remember this interior, the interior of all stores' backends. I would work in one, bringing stock from the walk-in out of boxes and onto refrigerator shelves, from behind. It was so obvious, that the drinks were all stored back there, waiting to be shoved frontwards, not delivered through the customer entrance, and yet I had not intuited the world behind each system. I have since become a project manager at the Jewel-Osco Headquarters in Itasca, working my way up through the stores, as you know. Still, I sometimes jump when I shop anywhere else and see a gloved hand emerging from behind the rows of beer boxes. Something about discovering that icy space, imagining its dimensions, its dim lighting and its cooler person in a dirty coat, even if I've been one, unsettles.

I sipped my coffee. As the phone on the other end rang, I remembered that I did not have a plan. "Hello?" said Norma, in a voice that was not necessarily panicked. I told her an elaborate story about Candy's father taking us shopping in the town over, an unplanned excursion, no phones for miles. I'd be back soon. She had been worried.

I hung up and, since I was there, called Candy.

The door to the office opened. It was Mickey and Doug, each holding a tall can of Colt 45. I asked Mickey, listening to the phone ring, how we were getting back to Grand Rapids.

"Not sure about that."

I wished, then, that being not sure was fine. That there was nothing drawing me anywhere. The days could keep running into each other and then when I did find my way down, it would be a trip, not home.

Cassie answered.

"Candy's in Berrylawn."

"What?" Work, death, psychosis. It had to be the last thing.

"She's fine. My dad thinks she tried to kill herself. She's fine."

"What did she do?"

"Lauren has a car," said Mickey, behind me.

"Oh, honey." Maybe Cassie could hear what Mickey had said. He pulled a piece of foiled paper from his pocket, dragging out a confetti of loose tobacco and a number in Lauren's fast and confident handwriting. I hated her. I hung up and dialed.

"Newaygo?" asked Lauren.

"Let me talk to her," said Mickey. He took the receiver. "Hey, we got something you'll want, I think." Lauren spoke and then Mickey said, "My buddy will give you directions."

Doug took the phone and started in on a set of highway numbers and distinctive landmarks he'd repeated a hundred times before.

Mickey turned to me, smiling. "Got you that ride. You do need it, right?"

"Yeah," I said, spinning. "Work." I didn't bring up Candy, saving her the dignity of proving him right, that she was "a little nuts." His eyelids were dark and soft. This off-limits space was his element. He scanned the room for things to steal.

Doug hung up. "She's gonna be at my place in two hours," he announced. "Just enough time to catch a flick." They hid the empty tall cans behind a hollow wall, stuffing three more full ones and a six pack into Doug's backpack on the way out. We walked past the café and thanked the woman again, who refilled our coffees "on the house."

I know Norma misses her giant house full of kids and a husband, wishes she'd said less to him to make him feel differently about her. Maybe she has a beer with breakfast in her condo. The last time I saw her, she drove to Meijer with a metal thermos in the cup holder, and I assumed it was full of vodka and lemonade and ice cubes from a machine in her refrigerator door. I picture us drifting into an intersection or rolling down a hill as she gestures at ways in which the suburbs have changed, million-dollar homes, a new place one of her sons seems to like. The boys occasionally come over for dinner, but they spend more time with their father because he is their boss.

At a bar, Candy and I sit and have a happy hour double well whiskey and Diet Coke with a basket of free popcorn. We would be the same as ever if it weren't for her always having a new boyfriend, one in a lineup of increasingly inconsequential men. They are people I'd never notice or know a thing about except that Candy describes their attributes and tastes to me, focusing on the positive, while they sit and drink. Her way of including them in conversation is asking for confirmation. "He loves that show, we watch it together, huh?" The man nods, raises his eyebrows, remembering something amusing. It's almost impressive, how much she can get out of such unremarkable people, how many she can find and shower with attention until they trust her, and she can let go again.

"He takes care of me, don't you," she says, rubbing the man on his back. He bristles, and, having drunk multiple shots of some mixture that appeared curdled, heaves, his shoulders spasming and his face reddening. "Hey," says Candy, rubbing faster, in small circles. I'm sitting on the other side of her, looking away, at a game on a mounted television set, at anything but the inevitable.

"Hey," she says, louder, and he vomits, a spray the color of snot soaking the bar, filling his half-empty glass of beer, clogging the rubber mat where empties are set to dry. A splatter coats the plastic lid of a tray full of citrus wedges. The bartender barely looks up. "Out," he says, whipping a rag over his shoulder, pointing to the front door.

Candy could argue that she should be able to stay, that we all should, that we aren't paying. She could jump over the counter and steal a bottle on her way out, as I've seen her do before. She could yell at her boyfriend, telling him he's a mess and a loser. She could cry, run to the bathroom, tell me to save her from the embarrassment of her life. I never know exactly what she will do, even after knowing her for so long. She sits up and looks at each person, eyes darting faster than we can comprehend, the way they did in high school: me, the bartender, me again, her boyfriend, who is staring at the floor and gripping his stool with both hands.

"Come on," she says, and then breaks into body-shaking laughter. Mortified, noticing the odor, I nod, unable to smile. She pretends to drop cash into the puddle and then catches it, hands it to bartender, who doesn't smile either.

"Gotta go," he says.

She puts her beautiful hands up, a theatrical surrender, jumping down from her seat and leading us out the entrance to my car. "That's us," she says, climbing into the passenger seat, "on a Tuesday."

The movie theater was a few parking lots over. Mickey had never heard of anything that was playing. Doug said he was better off. If we wanted in, we had to act fast, sneak through the exit as someone was leaving, walk quickly and silently through the nearest door inside. We shuffled through darkness, slumping the noisy backpack into its own seat. We had entered an action movie about aliens attacking the world. Whole continents lit up red from a satellite view, bombed to charred earth in seconds by spaceships miles away.

I turned to Mickey, who was bouncing his leg. He leaned sideways, toward me. "This movie is nuts," he whispered, staring at the screen. I thought of Candy again, alone in the hospital. There were maybe five people in the theater total. "I might go have a cigarette." I thought he would probably turn to kiss me then. Instead, he got up and lunged away. There was an empty seat between Doug and I now. He looked asleep. The firebombs were so impactful, they caused earthquakes and tsunamis, affecting land on the other side of the world, too. But America was being strategically saved so that the aliens could negotiate with the leaders of the free world amid chaos.

Mickey returned and Doug got up as soon as he sat down, shuffling past our knees. I psychically willed Mickey to kiss me, hold my elbow, squeeze my hip, but he was sinking into his chair, studying the movie carefully. A massive metal pole careened toward us, having been severed from a military boat. When it crashed into a yacht full of panicking rich people, Mickey's whole body stiffened. Doug came back to his seat.

"Now I gotta take a shit," whispered Mickey, who got up and left again.

Doug leaned over, bridging the chasm. "This movie is confusing."

I smiled. Then, realizing he couldn't see my face, I said, "Yeah."

Mickey came back and sat uncomfortably down. Doug asked if we wanted to leave or stay. Mickey took a deep, fast breath, and stood up again.

"Come on, man," said someone in the row behind us.

"Alright, alright, I'm going," growled Mickey in a voice that was both high and low. "Enjoy the *film*." We walked out single file.

Shielding our eyes from the sun with flattened hands, we walked past strips of tan businesses that shared marquees decorated with printed plastic slides: a local attorney, H&R Block, Enterprise, a hearing aid company, a chiropractor and acupuncturist, a chain tutoring program for kids in grade school, a dance studio. The signs looked impermanent, shifting out of their frames, bending to fit, but appeared as if they'd been there for decades.

Doug was talking about his parents, who wanted to retire in Florida. He was thinking about moving down with them. Mickey said his sister had moved to California and he was going to go there once it got cold again. "No point staying here," he said.

"That's a little insensitive, don't you think?" said Doug. He looked at me.

"Fuck Michigan."

"Iggy Pop is from here," I said.

"He lives in Florida now," said Doug.

"Hey, suckers." Lauren's Karmann Ghia slowed to a stop on our left.

My heart jumped into my throat when Mickey opened the passenger side door, but he was pulling the seat forward to get in the back.

When I visit from Chicago, Candy and I go for a ride to the lake or the grocery store or the nail salon or another bar. She's done with drama, she tells me, spinning in the passenger seat, looking at her boyfriend, me, the rearview mirror, the scenery that passes us. That's why she's dating such a "non-passionate" man.

"It's true," the boyfriend says from the backseat, "I have no passions."

"We never fight," says Candy, and I want to believe her. "Well, the last time he pissed me off, I saw something on his phone."

"We already went over this," says the boyfriend. "It's a long story," he says, touching the headrest on my seat. "We're past it now."

"We are," says Candy. She's not interested in figuring out if she can trust a person, she explains. If she can't, there isn't a point to questioning why. "Give up or get over it," she says, meaning no argument is worth it.

I do not tell them about the arguments I had with my ex, although I could, and maybe that would be kind of me. I do not mention when our neighbors called the cops on us, the lock that still isn't fixed on my door. I haven't told you about all that yet either. Maybe I should, or should have, on our first date.

Every time I'm back I remember that summer I lived there less, new memories painting over old ones, businesses taking over others, the city shifting and expanding. This could be the last time, if no one else gets married or dies, and it can finally be frozen instead of water to tread, in which darknesses I've forgotten bob up as drunken jokes, in which someone could easily tell me I got it all wrong.

"Remember the politician?" I ask.

Candy waits for me to finish the sentence and then understands that was the end of it. She says his name, which I had not immediately remembered. Her eyes are still darting, searching, now, for what I am thinking. How could I forget his name?

"Didn't he have a son?"

"Stephen," says Candy, quickly. "Yeah, Tess, his son, Stephen, who you had a massive crush on?"

Because I am driving, peering down a road that needs my attention, I can blink this away. Yes, I did know this. I would have had to. Candy turns around in her seat, mouth open. She is not convinced. I am not convinced. I will look it up later.

My mother had lived by the rules of karma: you get what you deserve. It was hard, now, to believe in that because she'd gotten a worse deal, unless there was some secret murder that I wasn't aware of. Sheila had not wanted to die, was not ready to, and denied that she would until the very end. Relying on karma, or some balance in the universe, had failed her.

In Civics, we were supposed to discuss different sides of a current controversy. No one wanted to dispute the pro-life movement, though. The thing that was wrong with the argument was that it used religious beliefs as evidence. But the thinking on the other side seemed to only use disdain for religious beliefs as theirs. The real reason I felt so strongly about the topic, probably, was that I would opt for an abortion if it ever came up. And that was a selfish reason, not an ethical one. Maybe self-centeredness was the reasoning behind every decision I made.

All our History class readings ended in an explanation that could really be boiled down to someone's religion, too. Everything was done or fought or defended because someone wanted goodness, which was subjective. We could agree that the Nazis were wrong. Ian's swastika tattoo was a big mistake, but he had an argument for it anyway.

"Where are we going?" Lauren asked. I turned around in my seat to look at the boys in the back. Doug leaned forward to lead the way. Mickey was like an actor, always looking into some distance. As we drove up to the trailer park, a woman emerged and stood in her doorway. A man came out of another trailer and folded his arms.

"Here come the freaks," Lauren yelled.

"Speak for yourself," said Doug. "I live here."

"You're a bigger freak than any of us," said Mickey.

We piled out of the car and into the house, which felt smaller now with Lauren there. The roommate or boyfriend never reappeared. I sat on the couch, desperate for something to own. I could stand over the sink and do the dishes now, and Mickey could do the thing I'd wanted him to do, putting his arms around me. He wouldn't, though. I wasn't that dumb, at least. If I could hint to him that I'd like to have sex now, he would take me into the other room. I did want to have sex, in fact, to feel his hands on my waist. I could see the smoke of his cigarette collecting in his hair afterwards, foam pulling through kelp in a tide pool.

I was there and I wasn't. Doug slapped one of his elbow pits. Lauren rolled up one sleeve and started to rub her arm, too. Mickey was silent and still. I went to the bathroom and waited. When I came back out, it appeared to be over, but no one was sprawled out onto the floor or nodding off. They were talking about what movie to put in the VCR. They settled on one about teenagers in the eighties, which transfixed me while everyone else drank beers and restlessly wandered around the little space, making toast, or going outside to smoke, or organizing the contents of the backpack. Every few seconds, I asked myself if it seemed like the right time to bring up leaving.

"Where's Ian?" asked Lauren, after she'd been there for hours.

"That guy thinks I owe him money," said Mickey, after a pause.

"That guy," said Lauren, in a louder voice, "owes *me* some fucking money."

"I should really get back," I said to Lauren, finally.

"I came all the way out here; I'm not leaving yet," she snapped.

It was dark out when we got back in the car. I started to fall asleep in the front seat, so while we were stopped at a gas station, Lauren told me that I could sit in the back if I wanted. I did. Mickey didn't move, and so Lauren was alone in the front, driving us home, high and drunk. I leaned my forehead on the cold window, but then Mickey took me by the shoulder and eased my head into his lap. He squeezed my hip. I could feel a pulse in his pants. My mouth was dry, and old sweat was glazing my clothes.

"Lance was fired," said Georgia, an RN, as I punched in for work. I didn't know who could fire Lance because he was our manager. He was the one telling me I was late when my card read 7:03 or stepping in front of me when I was carrying a heavy tray of coffee mugs to tell me I needed to go back into the storage room to put gloves on. "He was smoking crack in the damn parking lot." Georgia was backing up and holding her mouth with both hands. "Everyone knows he's a crackhead. That noise he makes with his throat."

Maybe he cleared his throat a lot, but I thought of it as a nervous tic. He didn't have the gelatinous eyes and dolphin gurgle of the crackhead that used to sway down my old street. Lance's breath smelled sour, and his teeth were striped yellow and gray, but he carried himself as if he were an attractive man, winking at all of us and joking with whoever was closest to him about his full and demanding social life.

"Who's the manager, then?"

"There isn't one."

"So, I don't have to be here?"

"Oh, the hell you don't. I'm not bussing tables just because they hired some crackhead for the kitchen. You don't wanna get paid?"

I blushed. Every time I talked to an RN she tried to get me to admit I didn't need my job. All the hostesses and dishwashers were high schoolers, and most of them lived in my neighborhood, meaning my aunt and uncle's neighborhood. I grabbed a hairnet and shuffled into the walk-in. Vanilla puddings in plastic stemmed cups were covered by a single sheet of Saran wrap.

Norma and John had been home when I was dropped off by Lauren. They watched as I made myself a peanut butter sandwich to take downstairs. I was just tired, I insisted, from swimming in the pool with Candy and Lauren, my two best friends. I had been mistaken about who would end up taking me home and when. I must have fallen asleep at some point, because then I was waking up, pulling myself out of bed, late for work.

"My daughter," said Betsy Van Derron. The reason I'd avoided Betsy was her propped up ankles, which were swollen past the width of her purple, socked feet, dimpled, like cellulite, and distended, like pregnancies. The rest of Betsy was thin: arms that crossed over a satin-hemmed blanket, a vacant face, and long, white hair. She was wheeled in feet-first and seated beside a table instead of at one because her legs were too high to go underneath.

"My daughter, come to visit," said Betsy again, in my direction. "Oh, how stupid of me. My daughter is twice your age."

I was used to these delusions, but not as quick to respond to them as the RNs, who could always change the subject to something happening at that moment or in the extremely near future.

"My daughter is going to visit me soon," said Betsy. "I just keep getting the days mixed up, since they're all the same." Candy was in one of these buildings, getting fed some pills in a paper cup, I assumed. "She looked a lot like you when she was younger. She looked just like me when I was younger, too." She lifted a hand to touch the top of her head. "I used to model, if you can imagine that."

"That's cool," I said. "What kind of modeling?"

"Oh, back then, there was only one kind. We went to a school for girls, the Barbizon Institute, and we walked with books balanced on our heads. We could do anything with books on our heads."

"I wish I could do that," I said.

"Oh, it was pointless, all of it."

I wondered if Betsy's swollen ankles were the only reason she couldn't be in the nicer home, Assisted Living. She seemed, despite having mistaken me for her middle-aged daughter, to have more presence of mind than the others.

"Did you travel?"

"Not really. Well? No."

I imagined what modeling meant in Grand Rapids: car showcases, department store catalogues, mall runways. Better than working at a nursing home. I imagined someone else walking into the dining room—the dish washer, the filmmaker, anyone—interrupting my conversation with Betsy about wasted youth and wasting mine. I had felt power over men only briefly, before they had seen through or past me.

On TV, the trophy wives were somehow the stars. They could get their husbands to give them rich lives, simply by being beautiful. Their beauty had faded but the agreement was in place. Maybe there were indiscretions, but in the end the knowledge remained: someone with a lot of money was willing to pay for a woman's entire life, simply because she had asked him to. The metal foot of a wheelchair slammed into my shin as Cal maneuvered to her seat. I crouched to hold the point of impact, sucking air.

"That book would be on the floor right now," said Betsy.

I clocked out and walked toward Psychiatric, knowing it had a fence that would stop me from getting anywhere near the building. There was a neighborhood of cul-de-sacs behind all the Berrylawn buildings. Some of the windows were so large, the rooms inside were visible from the winding sidewalks. Every house looked empty but in use. Their ceiling fans were solid shapes of motion. Their ovens were blurred with heated air. Their grass batted under sprinkler showers. Their dogs whined through glass doors.

From my room, I could hear people coming in and out of the house, being welcomed and introduced to other guests, opening bags of chips, pouring them into glass bowls, bringing handfuls of utensils outside for the Fourth of July cookout. I wrote in my diary, *If one more person asks if I'm okay or need something, I'm going to scream.*

The stairs to the basement chirped with the weight of small steps.

"Sorry," said a kid, one of my cousin's cousins. "Is the bathroom down here?"

"You can use that one," I said, pointing to mine.

Justin came down next. "What up," he said. "You seen Junior?"

I nodded at the bathroom. We stood at the foot of the stairs.

"I was gonna ask you." Justin looked at a point above my head. "You got, like, a hookup?" I stared at him. "For like, weed. Or whatever. For my friend."

"Sure," I lied.

"Just, you know, don't tell anyone, okay? Like, not even my brother. He would freak out. Everyone would freak out." He shook his head. "You must think we're so lame."

"That's not what I think at all."

"You should come upstairs. It's not so bad." He skipped steps going back.

Eventually, I was hungry enough to creep outside. I tried not to make eye contact with anyone on my way to the grill, where John was turning hotdogs and flipping burgers. He put a bun in my hand, cracked it open with the tongs, then wordlessly placed a dog in its center.

Norma snuck up behind me. "You almost missed the fireworks."

I sat cross-legged on the lawn, cousins throwing a football to one another. As the sky lit up, I wished that Candy was there, awed by the explosions that reminded us of the drugs trickling in our bodies. A bright point silently expanded and burst, glittering traces falling, a delayed crack. Each one was better than the last because we could only see the remnants of what was being replaced.

I'd forgotten to take my Prozac again. When it was working, I could sleep for fourteen hours or four and feel fine, watch the static wash over bad cable channels, a picture of kinetic energy. For a whole week, I heard radio signals in my fillings. Hours of my life were lost due to the ingestion of dextromethorphan, clonazepam, alprazolam, promethazine, codeine, oxycodone, alcohol mixed with fluoxetine and caffeine, a couple mystery drugs, and pressed pills. Every time I dissociated, it was either the start of a nervous disorder, a new side effect, or something working its way through my system from the night before. I'd held onto a concrete wall because I had to. I'd been taken to the school nurse, kept in a little room with a cool towel on my forehead. She let me stay for as long as I wanted. Mostly, she said, she dealt with liars.

I heard my uncle's brother say to him "some Dutch courage" as he handed off a beer. I knew that Dutch Masters were painters and also cigars, that drugs were legal in Amsterdam, and that dancing was illegal in the Dutch Reformed Church. When I asked my aunt about this contradiction, she seemed perplexed, and then, with an inside-joke smile, said, "Well, we must have left for a reason."

Again, I thought of Candy, alone, on a cot with plastic sheets, tears streaming from the outside corners of her eyes as she counted the dimples in a ceiling tile. The people I lived with and some people I'd never met discussed how well-done meat should get and what the best time to go out to the lake would be. Normally, they'd all be out there on pontoons today, but it was getting treated for some invasive toxin. When the sky was dark, I went down to my room to heat up a clothes hanger and press it against the back of my thigh until it went cold.

"I wanted to try something with you." Dr. Herman got up from his chair, opened a closet door I hadn't previously noticed, and walked out a tripod, on top of which sat a long panel of tiny lightbulbs, like a Lite-Brite with only one row. He had to kneel to plug it in and adjust the telescoping legs. He sat back down and then leaned over again to pick up a tiny remote connected by a wire.

The bulbs lit up blue, in order, a ticker moving from left to right, then back, from right to left. He told me to follow with my eyes.

"I want you to think about a time when you were feeling happy. Where are you? The first thing that comes to mind."

"Our house in Ypsilanti. My mom's."

"What are you doing there?"

"Making dinner."

"What are you making for dinner?"

"Baked potatoes with sour cream."

The light sped up and turned green. It bounced, rather than slinked.

"You're taking potatoes out of the oven. What is happening now?"

I couldn't hear myself. The light slowed down, and I followed it to a stop. When it was off, I was aware that my breathing had become heavy. My face was tight. I touched a cheek, and it was wet.

"How are you feeling?"

"Fine." I searched for a tremble.

Dr. Herman was asking more questions, but his voice was far away.

"Was I talking?" I asked.

He took off his glasses, polished bones, and put them on his desk. "I want you to know," he continued, "that coming to these sessions is entirely up to you."

"It is?"

"Of course."

"Oh." I picked up my purse and walked out into the hall, gently shutting the door behind me. I asked to use the phone at the front desk.

The office stretched as if behind a slamming screen door.

"I can call someone for you if it's an emergency. Do you feel sick?"

"No. My ride isn't here."

"Oh, it's not five yet." The receptionist lifted her thermos, the same kind Dr. Herman had, and I heard ice cubes in it, too. I sat in a chair and pictured his expression as I walked out. His office stayed shut. He could call a friend or read from a book, and I could do neither of those things. The wall's texture appeared different from different angles. In a painting of wildflowers, one of the lilac buds was not attached to its stalk.

A man emerged from another room holding a pack of cigarettes. He nodded to the receptionist. I followed him outside and asked for a cigarette. He snorted and looked at the sky. We were silent for a time. I opened my mouth, not sure if he had heard me.

"What's your story?"

"I'm just trying—"

"Aren't we all. Working out the details."

A cloud tilted, exposing the sun. I closed my eyes. "I'm on antidepressants," I said.

"Do you like being on anti-depressants?"

"Not really."

"Is there an alternative?"

"The generic?"

"No, like, can't you just, feel your own emotions?"

"Sometimes I feel something."

"Do you ever get really fucking angry?"

"Yeah."

"Oh yeah?"

"My best friend is in the mental hospital."

"I know all about those places."

"Something about it sounds nice."

"Sounds like you're not on the right meds."

It wasn't the politician's age that excited me, it was the conceit of showing my body to someone desperate to see it. I wanted to feel that desperation, up close, and I did, and it killed him.

At night before I fell asleep, I'd imagine disrobing, someone's hands trying to get my clothes off faster, on a loop. The hands might belong to boys I knew didn't like me. I'd sit on their laps and laugh at them. Once I'd had sex with Mickey, the fantasies were more difficult to conjure, interrupted by the realities of how it happened.

"I was getting to think you'd forgotten about me," messaged the politician, even though he was the one who had stopped signing on. "I'm coming to Grand Rapids tomorrow. We should meet."

He was still typing.

"There is a way out of this place, and I can show it to you if you give me a chance," he wrote. Was "this place" Grand Rapids? Was the "way out" Grosse Pointe?

When I called Candy's house, I must have been expecting to get her father or her sister, but I remember her answering, with a voice both familiar and changed, sort of afraid and bored at the same time.

We must have had a conversation about her anger at me for leaving her, for kissing Ian, for getting a ride back with Lauren, but I remember that she was happy to be on the phone with me.

The Amway Grand Plaza Hotel's façade and entrance is the restored Pantlind Hotel, built in 1913, an architectural emblem of ambition and what I still refer to as the most beautiful place I've ever entered, although I refuse to go back now to see if that's true. I remember its arched ceilings and ornate rugs, crystal chandeliers with lights the exact color of candle flames, everything curved and curling. Behind the Pantlind is a glass tower as tall as anything in the city and behind that, the green, churning river.

"Who's the group playing today?" asked Candy's father in my direction as he drove up the hill toward the highway.

"It's not about the music," said Candy.

"Pardon me, I thought you were blue fans."

At the bandshell, men on motorcycles pulled up and shoved their helmets off. We heard bass and the squeals of feedback, then cheers. It was still light out. The sky was gray but cloudless, as it somehow always was downtown. The air smelled of yeast and chlorine.

"I gotta ask you something," said a duck-footed woman with one arm in a sling. "Wait, how old are you?"

"Eighteen," said Candy, practicing our lie.

"You're a baby," she said. "You're nothing but babies. Have you seen a guy around here, he's the tallest man in the world, I swear. He drives one of them buses," she gestured behind her.

We shook our heads and kept walking.

"Wait," the woman called. "Can you help me out? I just got out of the hospital." When I turned around, she was unbuttoning the sling's strap and letting her arm fall out. Wads of soaked-though gauze sank to the pavement. A pointed shape, something white and porous, was protruding from the wound.

"We don't have any money," called Candy as she took my hand.

We crossed the gated park, in which a few men were dozing. This was a Saturday afternoon, so we could have easily run into friends or people we wished were our friends. Brightly lit chain restaurants were wedged into elegant structures originally designed for high socializing. Murals of craftspeople told us that Grand Rapids was once a furniture capital. Karaoke comedy clubs and galleries with paintings of dams replaced one another, footing offices and banks. The hotel took up a city block. The ramp to its entrance was carpeted.

A rectangular woman pulled on the front double door's handle, a golden, asparagus-shaped rod. She had to step back in her heels to disperse the suction. A man in a suit pushing a luggage cart left his post to help her inside. She trotted on block heels to a fountain ringed with velvet seats, where several men were waiting for her.

If we watched from outside for any longer, we would appear suspicious, I said.

"Go then," said Candy.

"He has to be good, for his image."

Candy made snoring sounds.

"I'm going in." I didn't move.

Candy walked past the man still holding the door and across the room, right up to the front desk. I followed. "Excuse me," she said. "I'm supposed to meet my father at the bar. Where is it?"

"There are two on this level and one on the balcony," said the receptionist, smiling.

We took the elevator with a man in a suit. He looked exhausted, like the skin around his eyes could rip. I was almost sure it wasn't him. No one spoke as the elevator slid up, chiming on each floor. Ladies first, the man gestured, but we had to let a guy carrying a domed metal tray pass. He nodded a thank you.

I scanned the bar, an open space lit by yellow sconces on dark wooden walls. No one was sitting alone. Another man in a suit had white hair and black-framed glasses. The "way out" was obviously being on television. This was an interview to see if we could move on from our lives to other ones. The man walked past us without stopping. Candy pulled me down the hall, yellow walls reflecting green carpet. She stopped and turned around. We kissed, and it occurred to me it was the first time outside of a home, unless we'd done something on one of the nights our memories were erased. We were back in the elevator. She pressed a random button, three. We kissed until we were on the third floor. The door opened to nothing. She pushed the Door Close button.

"What was it like?" I asked.

"You don't want to end up there."

"I didn't say I did."

"They wake you up just to give you a sedative. They make you sit in a room and do absolutely nothing. It's like solitary confinement. I watched *Mr. Holland's Opus* three times in three days, and that movie sucks. And then the group therapy. I don't think my dad knows how Christian it is there. It was my mom's idea to send Cassie. They read passages from the Bible. I mean, they quote the Bible, from memory, but it sounds like they're just talking, like this is just how people talk."

"That's—"

"Insane, I know. It probably makes people crazier. It's such a huge scam and a waste and a shit hole. I'm never letting anyone send me back there. Everyone is there to be punished, not to get better. I did meet this girl, though. She's fucking cool. She's not out yet but she knows where to get ecstasy."

The elevator opened to the lobby again and there he was, in a navy polo, belted khakis, leather-laced boat shoes. The tip of his nose was outlined in a peeling tan.

He knew it was us, although now I don't know how that would be. Had I ever sent him a photo? Did I even know how to do that back then? He stepped in among the dulled mirrors. "And you brought your friend." He pressed eleven. "Do you mind if we stop at my room?" He was looking up at the numbers as they changed, and we were looking at each other. "We can decide from there what we'd like to do." The door opened once more, and he led the way.

The room was nicer than any I'd seen, but I'd pictured something more elaborate after seeing the lobby. Candy opened the thicker curtain, letting sunlight through a sheer white layer. The politician filled in every empty second: the weather, the airport, the front desk service, the way his shoes squeaked, moving around the bed and sofa, distracting us from his physical body, a lingering odor of coffee, clothes made stale from being sealed in a suitcase. He kept smiling to himself, looking away and then, slowly, gently, at one of us. "Well," he said, hand on heart. "Listen to me. Would either of you like something to drink? How about I make us some cocktails? It is the weekend, after all."

We sat at the edge of the bed and nodded.

"Any preferences?" He opened the minifridge door and pulled each bottle up from its stall, recognizing the colors of labels.

"I'll have a martini," said Candy. I knew she'd always wanted to say that.

"There's an idea. You know, it's sort of magic, how making liquor that cold turns it into something new," he was talking into the fridge, opening the smaller door that was a freezer section. "And you know, it's somehow appropriate for all times of day, for all times of night, isn't it? Well, I'll have to order those from the bar, seeing as we have no utensils to fashion them. I'm saying 'them' because I believe I'll join you in this selection, a martini. And what about you, my dear? Would you like something different?"

"No," I said, knowing he was talking to me even though he hadn't said a name. Maybe didn't know which one I was. Maybe he thought I was Gina, the friend with whom I'd started chatting with him so long ago, when we were completely different people.

Gina only came to life online. Even though her family gave her everything, like tennis lessons and a blue-eyed white kitten and her own phone line, she wore stained clothing, hardly brushed her hair, answered on the first ring, saying, "I am literally doing nothing right now."

"What's that?" asked the politician, who did have a name, one that was everywhere, on signs in people's yards.

"Yes, I'd like a martini." It made me smile, like saying cheese.

"Martinis for all." Almost hopping, he made for the phone, picked up the receiver, dialed two buttons. "Yes, room service? Three martinis, gin, dirty," he paused, asking us if this was the correct order by sucking both lips behind his teeth and looking at each of us. We nodded. He hung up. "Oh, it's a hot one, isn't it?" He had said this already.

"It's freezing," said Candy.

"Isn't air conditioning incredible? What would we do without it?"

"A blast," said Candy.

"Oh, there you go. I got that one." They went on like this, tossing the topic of why we were here like a game of hot potato.

The politician blocked us with his body when he opened the door. A quiet exchange of words and money. On a tray, three conical glasses were filled to their brims with oily liquid and skewered olives.

"I hope you're hungry." We were alone again. He set the tray down on a dresser. Candy reached out with both hands, took a long sip, and made a sneeze-like sound from the back of her throat.

"It's not the best one I've ever had either. Would you like something else?"

"No."

I tasted mine. It was cold and then warm, and salty, like the water in Lake Michigan, but the alcohol cut through like the smell of a clean toilet.

"My father used to drink these," said the politician, settling into an armchair. "Out of a pitcher. He had this bar cart full of bottles, but he only ever drank from one, from the bottle of gin, when he'd make a whole pitcher of martinis."

"My dad only drinks beer," said Candy. "He's not this sophisticated."

"Oh, beer is a fine drink, too. Sometimes there's nothing better." They started up again, winding around each other in conversation, sloshing their glasses. "My father was such a closed book; I don't even know which way he voted."

"My dad tells me too much, like if he thinks our waitress is sexy."

"I would want to know that. I don't know why I would, but I think I would."

I stared into the bottom of my little pond of liquor, the olives like turtles trying to climb out. "My dad," I heard myself say.

"Is he a good one, or a not so good one? Aren't they all just a little bit awful?"

"Yeah," I answered. "Yeah." I was imagining another guy, some actor I'd cast to play my dad, not the real one. He was driving away, revving an engine. "My mom didn't like him so much."

"We should go to the pool," suggested Candy.

"It didn't appear to be open," said the politician, and they'd moved on.

"My friend wants to kiss you," blurted Candy, interrupting something he was in the middle of explaining, something that had put me into a trance.

"Well." He sipped. "Well."

"What if we both do?" asked Candy. She stood.

"What would two enchanting young women see in little old me?"

The game had paused, another started, one we'd all played before, even if we hadn't. This one I'd been waiting for, between the powerful and the young, after all the back and forth, had arrived lukewarm. Candy sat on one arm of his chair. I rose from the bed and took a step, set my drink down, took another step, sat on the other arm. She was already feeling for a belt buckle. The word *Would* repeated itself in my head.

"Oh," he inched his hips back. "Not right now. I'm having some issues in that area. Nothing to do with you." He looked at me. "Sorry about that, dears." I didn't understand why he thought we'd be disappointed. I could feel his breath on my cheek.

He stopped talking and started giving directions. His hands, now strong, turned our chins toward each other's. We kissed. He kissed our shoulders, our necks, pulled our shirts up. He sucked on Candy's nipple. He looked like a baby, eyes closed, lips distended. I wondered if I looked like that, with her.

We had climbed all over each other and him and the chair until he was exhausted, panting, but he didn't seem that bad. We never would have left if we had known he was in trouble. We loved him, we told each other, later. When we finally left, the sun had set. We held hands down the hallway and stepped back onto the elevator very drunk. We decided, in many words, that this type of thing would be our new way of life.

It was two whole days later when we saw him on the news. It was that same photo they always used, and then a video of his wife getting into a car, looking lost. I had to pretend, again, that I did not know him, while my family spoke about each of their inane lives, drowning out the television.

I sometimes confuse the details of losing my virginity. It was that entire summer; it was Lauren burning a hole in my arm. It was a bush and a bed and a hotel room and a trailer and looking at myself in the mirror for so long the shapes that made up my face would spread apart, sparkle. It was a death, and not the first one.

My mother would have said it didn't matter. She would have let me choose the time I thought it counted. She would have said it wasn't our fault, that the man had a heart condition, and we couldn't have known. I had no idea what my mother would have said and still don't.

I was on thin ice, and I knew it. Norma and John were planning something for me, to make sure I couldn't keep doing whatever it was I did. They were supposed to be keeping me away from all the bad stuff back home, from the waywardness of a single absentee father arrangement, and here I was, sleeping with junkies, getting high, murdering old men, having lesbian sex.

I covered the last table with its burgundy cloth and went back to the kitchen to retrieve lunch trays, which were in a line, each marked with a laminated name card on a spiraled metal stand. I put water or hot water or thickened water or Lipton in plastic cups, according to who liked what. I folded napkins and bibs and placed utensils into them or not. The line cook plated food as I watched from a window in the wall. She finished each setting with a lidded dish.

One tray was set aside, with only the sippy cup I'd filled and its name card on it. Genie Kemp. That gesture: the stupid empty tray being moved off the line. I asked the cook to be sure. "Is Genie Kemp gone?"

"You gotta get used to that here." I took the other trays to their places. Whether I'd seen the tray moved aside or not, I would have noticed her absence, I was sure. One of the women cried out. Another made a grunting sound that was maybe meant as polite laughter. A chapped plastic bowl bounced out of an RN's hands as Mrs. Holt grinned, an admission that the disruption had been intentional. The RN ripped off her apron and left it on the chair. Mrs. Holt had wanted, as an infant does, for things to go in a new direction.

After lunch, I scrubbed the dried splash of oatmeal off where it had seeped through the cloth and onto the laminate table. One of the dish washers stood in a corner, waiting for me to finish, watching me. I arched my back as I scrubbed, then dipped the washcloth into a bucket of soapy water that was getting cold. I felt all my movements, the muscles in my arms, the young man's eyes on them. When I turned around, though, he wasn't there anymore.

When I hurried through a shift, the RNs looked at me with straight mouths. One day I would learn that everyone can't just leave that place when the work was done, that some people wake up there every morning and sleep there every night.

In the back of Lauren's car, colors and patterns showed through plastic bags—red gingham, brown and purple marble, embroidered patches on light blue denim, the undeniable green of a Girl Scout vest, a fluorescent pink sports bra, a fluffy messenger bag in Smurf blue—barely masked remnants of her previous phases. She was wearing what she wore when she picked us up in Newaygo. The idea had never occurred to me, to wear the same thing every day. Mickey had a uniform, too. A soft white shirt, stiff black jeans, salty tattoos.

We had to stop at a yellowing house with broken porch steps. Inside, the walls were painted a spectrum of blues behind delicate, pointed stars. "Stephen did those," said Lauren, rushing past the front room. "Cool, right?"

I stayed where I was, watching people in studded belts, glassy-eyed, holding forties and cigarettes and cans of hairspray, shuffling up and down stairs.

"It's got religious idolatry, but I'll allow it, since the intentions align with my philosophies." Someone was talking to me, pointing at a gold-rimmed portrait of the Virgin Mary positioned near the ceiling, where the sky darkened to midnight. "That's in homage to the artists hired by Catholics to decorate their churches, which are, let's face it, the great masterpieces of human history. They were a joint effort: artists desperate for money, and everyone else, desperate for salvation. Were you at the wake?"

I stared at him, not understanding.

"The wake, for Caesar. I guess not. Thought I saw you there."

"No," I said.

"So, you didn't know Glen?"

"Glen?"

"Or Caesar? The wake was for Caesar, but Glen OD'd at it. You didn't hear about this? Dude, Glen was the best. I'm Mark."

Lauren was back.

"Did you know Glen?" I asked.

"Not until Caesar's wake," said Lauren.

"He was depressed," said Mark.

"Who isn't?" asked Lauren. Mark shook his head and stomped up the stairs, grasping a noisy wooden banister. No one said anything as we left through the front door and got back into Lauren's car. Before she'd turned the engine on, another guy from inside came out onto the porch and spit off the side onto the dirt, then wiped his mouth and went back in.

Lauren paid for parking downtown with her credit card but told me I owed her. "Rose! Fallon!" she yelled into cupped hands getting out of her car. Rose's pants were low enough to show a tattooed garland of roses across her hips. The four of us walked in the same direction for a time.

"Heard of anything going on tonight?"

"We're getting up super early tomorrow."

"Sucks. Why?"

"We're counselors."

"Community service?"

"I take this youth group camping in the UP every summer," said Rose. "This is Fallon's first time coming with."

Fallon was holding her hands together at her chest. "I'm so excited."

As we separated, I said to Lauren, "Was that for real?"

"Basically, it's like, most people here are into Jesus." I pictured them at church, talking to the boys with the mirrored sunglasses. Maybe there was another, cooler, cool church.

Lauren saw Mickey first. She stretched her arms out and he tilted his head back, catching her embrace. She even bent her knees and kicked up her feet, hanging from Mickey's neck as he tried to keep his cigarette away from her face. Then Candy appeared and shot through the hug, knocking them each off balance. She aimed a fist at Mickey's cheek. Once, twice, a sound like a heartbeat, like it could last a lifetime, then his hands were on her shoulders, arms locked. People stopped and gathered to watch. "Oh, shit," said a guy's voice. Lauren rocked herself up off the pavement, saying, "What the fuck," again and again. I was calling Candy's name, telling her to stop. And then Sadie was there, separating everyone. It was over in seconds.

"Fuck, I guess she really is nuts," Lauren said to Mickey, who was looking at Sadie and touching his cheek.

"You're on your own, sweetheart," Sadie said over her shoulder at me.

"You know what?" said Lauren, suddenly more animated than I'd ever seen her. "Fuck this." She looked at me. "You're not using me for my car anymore."

Mickey and Sadie had already started walking away, and then Mickey stopped, turned around, and looked at Candy, then at me. "I did care," he said, as if translating the words from another language. What did he mean? What kinds of movies did he watch when it was up to him? Where were his parents from? I didn't know Mickey, and so I will always love him.

The crowd dispersed to reveal the usual couples getting drunk while their kids begged for treats from carts. I recognized the woman with the broken arm from the bus stop, but she was unscarred. The Great Dane was walking around again off-leash, letting his snout gently fold and drag as he sniffed the rugs selling beeswax soaps, windmill cookie tins, handmade clay pots stuffed with African violets in soil.

"I bet you gave him a black eye," I said.

"I don't give a shit," said Candy.

"He called me stupid."

It was the best way things could have ended. Before long, he was dating Lauren for real, for years. They even lived together in a house with roommates, long after I'd gone back to Ypsi. I thought of them when I tried heroin for the first and last time, just to see what it was like. I made my line extra thin. I felt the same rush as when cough syrup was working, the same tingle as the time right before falling asleep. Someone described it as life suspended, like knowing you'd never know pain again. I thought it was nice, and that was about it.

"Can we go see the fish ladder?" Candy asked, and we walked to the river. It looked like the steps in front of the public library, but underwater. Candy read the plaque to me. It was created to circumvent other manmade barriers to a fish's natural migration patterns. The river was too strong, and the fish needed this shortcut. It was ugly, we agreed, and the fish were ridiculous, catapulting up each level, flopping in the air.

Bella announces she is pregnant, again. Everyone seems surprised, since her husband is never filmed, and so we have forgotten his existence. We assumed, we must admit, that he is a bad person, sneaking around like that and leaving his wife to do all the talking.

"Next time, on *Grosse Income*," says a narrator. In an edited version of the final episode of the season, Rachel's husband is on trial. He could be sentenced for many years in prison, we learn, from a conversation between everyone excluding Rachel, over large creamy cocktails in drop-shaped glasses. Bella puts a maraschino cherry into her mouth and yanks at its stem. "It's gonna be . . . not nothing."

"Fraud," says a chorus, in unison. "Fraud," Bella repeats, leaning closer to Patricia, who winces. Here, the clip slows down. A hollow sound effect lines up with a zoom-in. The glass is quickly emptying of white liquid and the ice cubes in it are becoming exposed.

Rachel is in a living room, crying. Her friends take turns putting a hand on her back. Patricia says: "I thought that divorce was going to leave me with less options, but it has done the opposite."

"I don't want more options." Rachel takes her head out of her hands.

A friend, Maureen, is visiting from a houseboat in Amsterdam. "Let me say this," she says. "I'm so, so, so, so, so, so, glad I grew up here. It is priceless, to be from a place as wholesome, and just, you know, honest, as Michigan."

"But you're not raising *your* kids here," says Rachel.

"We want them to be cultured. It's my husband's opinion."

"Ex-husband."

"Sometimes I forget."

"She thinks she has something over us."

"Look, when I say something, I mean it." A wild look lands on Maureen like the darkness from a setting sun. She stabs her fork into a piece of steak on Rachel's plate and suspends it. The camera's lens has trouble focusing on the meat. This behavior looks strange and disgusting because everyone else is sitting up straight and holding, if anything, a glass, poised to interject. The steak is getting ready to weep some sauce. She puts it down and raises her shoulders. From this gesture we can see that Maureen, a new character introduced in the series' last episode of the year, which turns out to be the last episode ever, is feeling something. We can see, just by looking at her wet eyes, that coming home has made her more homesick.

Mostly Sheila's diary is about things I could never recognize, like students in her classes, some landmark in an unnamed city, details that were both vague and labored. I should have pored over it, but sometimes I skimmed.

Happy to be moving where there are horses, she wrote. The horses were so close, you could hear them galloping from anywhere in the house. They would sometimes gather and run in a circle, pounding the dirt until it became dust. *Horseback was my best escape when I was her age. Like riding a bike, I hope. Let me get away from dad and all that.* I had to imagine she meant her own father, as in when she was around my age, although she could also have meant that once she got to Grand Rapids, she could take her sister's neighbor's horses out and it would all come back, and she'd be escaping my father, then.

Having a kid is the hardest thing, she also wrote, sometime around when we were moving. *It's like they want you to be them, for the harder parts. Like I can make living easier for her. I'm doing her a favor by taking her away from that place.* There it was. That unravelling, tightening pain. That dip in a succession of deeper and deeper dips. *I never thought I'd have to make so many decisions. Can't wait for this part to be over.* I closed the cover and put my head down into my chest, held a pillow in my bed with both arms and both legs.

Once, Sheila caught me with vodka on my breath. I came home from Mari's and talked for too long with her in the kitchen and she leaned in and sniffed. Then she smirked and said, "It isn't even that fun, is it?" with a face like she was angrier at herself than she was at me. I could only recognize the drooping eyes and inverted smile of drunkenness on her in retrospect, once I'd been drunk myself and looked in the mirror. I never thought of my mother as pretty or not pretty. Anyway, I looked more like my father.

At her funeral, I was the only person that audibly cried. It surprised even me. Someone handed me a tissue. I can see the stone gray of the walls, the glowing pink of the carnations, the small urn on a table draped with a teal tablecloth, like something from an Indian restaurant. On an easel, a blown-up photograph from five or seven years ago showed Sheila making a face I almost never saw: holding in laughter. It was taken on a vacation with one of her friends. I must have stayed home with my father then, although I had no memory of that part, only that she had been gone a long time, and I had missed her.

Norma went up to the podium and said a few things in a tearful voice, the voice of someone who wanted us to know she had already cried. She read from a piece of paper, a letter: "I believe, more than ever, in Jesus Christ," she read. It was something Sheila never said to me. My father must have been there, somewhere, but not in the front row with me. I didn't make a speech. The idea of speaking never crossed my mind.

I tried fentanyl a few months ago, knowing it was one of the drugs that they put Sheila on when she was dying. This guy had a whole sheet that he cut into individual patches for us to adhere to our bodies and let the drug be absorbed through our skin. Because it was so indirect, coming from this transparent rubbery gel sticker, like a comforting shoe insert, I assumed the effect would be mild. Instead, I felt higher than I'd ever been in my life.

The sky was smeared while the air stayed crisp, the sounds of ambulances echoing like trance music, the smells of an outdoor grill like a warm home. The guy put his arm around me, and we smiled into bright, loving eyes, while our friends who were too afraid to use the patches told us we looked slack and scary, "instant junkies."

We went to a house party and a fight broke out. We were dissociating, but we were not, importantly, hallucinating. All of this was real: the man lifting a wooden chair over his head, the bottle of tequila upending and soaking a couch. Nothing was a metaphor; the world was crashing down. He protected me, used his forearm as a shield and got us out of there, then kissed me, our mouths melting. This was before I met you. We stared at stars behind power lines and felt their orbits. Instead of the stupid pontificating that comes with psychedelics, we mostly laughed and mumbled, reiterating that the feeling was itself incredible.

"A killer of pain," I said.

"This is what they mean by getting high," he said, sounding completely lucid. The sensation of being alive can be heightened if it is almost escaped. There is a base, and one could rise over it, get up above the garbage, so far away you can't see the dirt in all the corners of the floorboards, the dust that has been painted over by the building's super so it will be there forever. "You can't lose if you don't try" is something I'd started to say often and so I whispered it in his ear, not meaning to sound like such a vampire.

We took the patches off before going to sleep, afraid we wouldn't wake up if we didn't. The contrast between the smudged landscape at night and this high-definition place in un-shadowed morning—my messy bedroom with a plate on the dresser, stale cigarette smell as opposed to fresh, earthy tobacco—made clearer the notion that every time I get fucked up in whatever way, I am creating distances, not getting closer to anyone or anything. This is an objective fact about which I feel completely neutral. I don't need to ever take fentanyl again but have no regrets. "Whatever," I said to the dozing person next to me, "if everything is a distraction, nothing is."

I redyed my hair black the day my father picked me up from my aunt and uncle's. As it dried, I saw the ends fold at sharp angles and threaten to split. It was hot, but I wore long sleeves and pants to cover my scabs. "Hey," he said, his voice shaky. "I sure missed you."

"Everyone is at church," I said. I wasn't aware, yet, that they had planned that. They were giving me back, the experiment having gone wrong. Grand Rapids and Berrylawn and Crescent Hills and Sundays and Christmas stockings and barbecues would soon be washed out, their colors drained. I ran down to my bedroom and grabbed the weekend bag I'd packed. The metal box in it rattled. I took one Prozac pill and a Dexatrim tablet I'd stolen from the grocery store. I ran back up and out the door, to the driveway. We got into his old station wagon, which smelled like my old life.

"Nice 'do," said my dad, rubbing the top of my head. I smoothed my hair back down. We were quiet for a while on the road. Teeth clenched, I started to point out the landmarks: where I got on the school bus, where we shopped, where I worked, the mental hospital, the exit to downtown. I didn't point out where Sheila had died. Then we were on the highway. He tuned the radio dial until he found a song he liked. At a commercial break, I asked if I could put a CD in. It was another mix Candy had made for me. I was surprised that he recognized some of the songs. I wondered if Sheila would have, too.

"She's my best friend," I said.

My father looked older than I remembered, more delicate around the mouth, with whiskery eyebrows. "I bet you hear people tell you that these are the best years of your life. They weren't the best years of my life."

I chewed on the sides of my tongue. Words piled up behind my mouth. This was why people smoked cigarettes, to stop themselves from saying nothing. Through the passenger side window, a slick of green spilled sideways, over an asphalt gutter. The trees were so tall I couldn't see the sky. Storm fences became tangled with vines and graffitied; concrete barriers became rust-stained and busted apart by ugly roots. A mass of fallen branches became like hair collecting around a bathtub drain, suctioned and spiraling, the gasping sound of a stream interrupted by air. Every bone in my body was suspended in a liquid, held by muscle. The car was not rolling but being ripped through time. Inside it were a million little screams that made one humming sound. My chest rose with each breath, my firm breasts, so enticing they'd stopped a man's heart. I didn't know yet that I was moving back home, but sensed, perhaps, that Grand Rapids was a nightmare from which I was waking.

Acknowledgements

Special thanks to Amelia Atlas, Patrick deWitt, Danny Gallegos, Naomi Huffman, Chris Kraus, Kaitlin Phillips, Julia Ringo, Sonia Stagg, Janique Vigier, Emily Westbrook, and Yaddo

ABOUT THE AUTHOR

Natasha Stagg is the author of *Surveys: A Novel* (2016), *Sleeveless: Fashion, Image, Media, New York 2011–2019* (2019), and *Artless: Stories 2019–2023* (2023). She lives in New York City.